# "I'm not beautiful, Ally said.

"Men don't—well, until I spent that night with you, I'd never slept with anyone else but my husband."

"Which proves what, exactly?" Raul asked.

"Which proves—that apart from being too old for you, I'm not the kind of woman that—that any man would—"

"You're talking rubbish," said Raul impatiently and, although she tried to evade him, he grabbed her arm and forced her round to face her reflection in the narrow mirror behind her. "Look at yourself," he commanded. "What do you see? Not the homely housewife you're describing, is it? Be honest with yourself, Ally. You're a lovely, passionate woman. Age doesn't come into it. You're in your prime. Accept it. Enjoy it."

# Anne Mather

## ALL NIGHT LONG

### *Passion*™

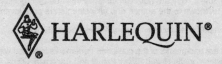

# HARLEQUIN®

TORONTO • NEW YORK • LONDON
AMSTERDAM • PARIS • SYDNEY • HAMBURG
STOCKHOLM • ATHENS • TOKYO • MILAN • MADRID
PRAGUE • WARSAW • BUDAPEST • AUCKLAND

ISBN 0-373-12170-9

ALL NIGHT LONG

First North American Publication 2001.

Visit us at www.eHarlequin.com

**Printed in U.S.A.**

# CHAPTER ONE

THE man *was* watching her.

Ally shifted a little uncomfortably on her stool at the bar and transferred her attention to the tall glass in front of her. Despite the fact that she had come down to the bar with the avowed intention of flirting with the first attractive man she saw, the reality was proving rather more daunting than she had anticipated. Besides, although she was almost sure he was watching her, he could be staring at something over her shoulder. Young men like him did not usually waste their time with middle-aged divorcees, particularly when the divorcee in question looked considerably the worse for wear.

Ally heaved a deep sigh and permitted herself another surreptitious glance in his direction. This time she caught his eye and she could feel the heat surge into her cheeks as she quickly looked away.

Dear God, she thought, picking up her glass and taking a reinforcing gulp of her vodka and tonic. He was watching her. But why? Surely he couldn't think she was a wealthy tourist, not with her cheap jewellery and chain store clothes.

She took a steadying breath. The trouble was, she wasn't used to this. It was twenty years since she'd been an active member of the singles scene and she had no idea how to cope with such an obvious appraisal. All right, she'd been fairly satisfied with her appearance when she'd looked in the mirror of the hotel room vanity unit upstairs, but she didn't kid herself that her brown hair—which had been decently cut and styled and streaked with blond highlights—or her decidedly unmodel-like figure were the stuff of any man's erotic dream. She was—or rather, she had been—a wife and

5

mother for too many years to start regarding herself as an attractive single woman again.

But that was why she was here, she reminded herself. Why she was spending the night at this luxurious hotel at Heathrow Airport before boarding the morning flight to Nassau and from there to the tiny island of San Cristobál. This holiday was intended to be her opportunity to escape— at least for a few weeks—from the pain and humiliation of the past year. And if, by going to stay with Suzanne, she was falling short of making a complete break from everything and everyone she knew, she was doing something she had never done before.

So why was she behaving so coyly, just because some man—some *strange* man—was showing interest in her? It wasn't as if she was likely to see him again after tonight. And, besides, he was far too young for her. If he was watching her, it was probably just curiosity. She looked so out of place here; he was no doubt wondering what she was doing out alone.

'Is this yours?'

She started at the voice. Despite her awareness of the man at the other end of the bar, she'd been completely wrapped in her thoughts, and the low appealing enquiry came as a total surprise to her.

It was him. As she'd been absorbed in finding reasons why he wouldn't be interested in her, he'd left his stool and was now propped against the bar beside her, her black clutch bag in his hand.

'Oh—' How had he taken possession of her handbag without her being aware of it? 'I—yes. Yes, it's mine.' She fairly snatched the bag from his outstretched fingers. 'Thank you.'

'No problem.' His voice had a faintly mocking tone as if he found her rather ungracious acceptance of his kindness amusing. 'It was on the floor.'

'Was it?' Too late. Ally remembered her elbow brushing

something as she'd swung round in her seat. 'Well, I'm very grateful. I'd hate to have lost it.'

Which was so true. Her traveller's cheques, her passport, and her air tickets were all in the bag. She'd been too nervous to leave them locked in her suitcase in her room.

'Accidents happen,' he responded lightly, his dark eyes appraising her with discomforting intensity. 'Are you waiting for your husband?'

*Her husband?*

Ally somehow suppressed the desire to laugh. It would have been slightly hysterical laughter, she thought bitterly, and she had no desire to show herself up in front of such a disturbing—and she sensed sophisticated—individual.

So, 'No,' she replied, with what she hoped was cool assurance. 'I'm not waiting for my husband.'

'Then can I buy you a drink?' he asked, nodding towards her almost empty glass. 'Vodka, isn't it?'

Ally's jaw was in danger of dropping and she hastily pressed her lips together. 'I—why—well, that's very kind of you, but—'

'But you don't know me from Adam,' he suggested softly, easing his hip onto the stool beside hers. 'Well, that's easily remedied. My name's Raul. What's yours?'

Ally hesitated. Raul, she thought, liking the sound of it. But, just Raul. Not Raul whatever-his-surname-was. It seemed that he had no more desire to betray his identity than she did, and while that should please her, it didn't.

'Um—I'm Diana,' she said, choosing a name at random. 'Diana—Morrison.'

'Hello, Diana.' His thin lips curled into an engaging smile. 'So—can I buy you a drink, Diana?'

Ally swallowed her disappointment that he hadn't chosen to be any more forthcoming, and cautiously inclined her head. 'Why not?' she said steadily. 'Thank you.'

He summoned the bartender with considerably less effort than she'd needed earlier and ordered her another vodka and tonic and himself Scotch over ice. Listening to him order the drinks, Ally wondered if he was an American, but although his accent wasn't wholly familiar, she sensed it wasn't a transatlantic drawl.

But it was an attractive accent, she conceded. Just as he was one of the most attractive men she had seen in her life. He was very dark-skinned, with lean, tanned features that had a faintly aquiline severity. But his mouth was far from severe. It had a decidedly humorous twist to the sensual lower lip, and his very dark hair made her wonder if he had any southern European blood in his veins.

She felt a slightly incredulous twinge that he should actually be buying her a drink. In her experience, men seldom came on to her, and just because her dress had a rather more daring neckline than usual, and she'd had her hair professionally styled, it did not mean she was any less the ugly duckling. There had to be some other reason why he was showing an interest in her, and she couldn't help worrying that she might not be experienced enough to cope with it, whatever it was.

What did she know of men, after all? Precious little, she acknowledged ruefully. She'd married Jeff soon after leaving school and for eighteen years after that she'd been too busy juggling the tasks of supporting him though his university days and raising the twins to pay much attention to anything else.

'There you go.'

The barman had returned with their drinks and Raul, if that really was his name, was pushing her glass towards her. Perhaps with a couple more of these inside her she'd feel a little less anxious, she thought hopefully, obediently raising her glass to her lips and forcing herself not to drop her gaze when he caught her eyes across the rim of his glass.

But it didn't last.

'I guess it's okay.'

His lazy comment made her realise that she'd swallowed

at least a third of the drink in one gulp and she hurriedly replaced it on the bar. 'I wasn't thinking,' she said foolishly, her nervous fingers toying with the edge of her coaster. She concentrated on setting the glass more centrally on the small mat. 'It's very nice.'

'Good.' He set his own glass down and she was supremely aware of his dark gaze assessing her averted face. Then, his breath fanning her hot cheek, 'Do I make you nervous?'

Ally sucked in a breath. 'Why should you think that?' she demanded, indignation giving her voice more confidence, and he sighed.

'I suppose because I get the impression that you're not used to—well, to this.'

'Picking up men in bars, do you mean?' she asked, controlling the instinct to confirm his suspicions and walk out of the bar with some difficulty. 'No, I'm not. Are you?'

'Used to picking up men in bars?' he echoed mildly. 'Hardly.'

'You know what I meant,' she accused him hotly. 'Now you're making fun of me.'

'No, I'm not.' And then, seeing her disbelief, 'Well, possibly. Just a little.' His smile was rueful as he picked up his drink. 'I'm just trying to get you to relax, that's all.'

'By asking me if I'm nervous?' Ally was scornful. 'I'm self-conscious enough as it is without you making me feel worse.'

The cuff of his blouson jacket brushed sensuously against her bare arm as he set his glass down again. It was made of soft leather, fine and expensive, and she couldn't prevent a shiver from sliding down her spine at the involuntary touch. It was black, like his hair, and beneath its folds a black tee shirt outlined the taut muscles of his flat stomach.

Ally caught her breath. Jeff would never have dreamt of wearing anything so casual in the evening, she reflected. A dark suit—latterly he'd been buying himself Armani, only

Ally hadn't been aware of it until— She discarded that thought before it could hurt her and moved on. A blazer, a sports coat—Harris tweed for preference—those were the things she was used to. But Raul looked as elegant in black jeans as Jeff had ever looked in his designer gear. But then Raul's clothes were obviously designer-made, too...

'Tell me why you're self-conscious,' he said, distracting her from her covert appraisal of his appearance. 'You have nothing to be self-conscious about.'

'No?' Ally stifled the snort that rose into her throat. 'Well, as you so succinctly remarked earlier, I'm not used to this— this scene.'

'What scene?'

'This scene.' Ally permitted herself to look at him for a moment and then expanded her gaze to include the whole room. 'Women sitting in bars on their own, accepting drinks from total strangers.'

'We're not total strangers.' He kept a perfectly straight face but she was sure he was laughing at her. 'We've been introduced.'

'We introduced ourselves,' Ally amended wryly. 'That's not the same thing at all.'

'Okay.' He conceded her point. 'But it's moot now, anyway. You can hardly pretend we don't know one another when you've just swallowed half the drink I paid for.'

Ally's lips parted. 'Are you implying I can't buy my own drinks?'

'Of course not.' He was evidently growing weary of her argument. 'Look, I'm sorry if I embarrassed you, right? I didn't mean to. I just wanted us to get to know one another better, and I foolishly thought that teasing you might do it.' He held up his hands, palm outward. 'Obviously, I was wrong.'

Now Ally felt sorry. She hadn't wanted to offend him, and it wasn't his fault that she was out of date when it came to dealing with the opposite sex. If anyone was to blame, she was. She had allowed Jeff to control her life for so long that she'd forgotten how to have fun.

'I'm sorry,' she said quietly, half surprised that he hadn't moved away to try his luck with someone else. There was certainly no shortage of younger—and apparently unattached—women in the bar, and from the looks she'd been getting, Ally guessed they were speculating about why a man like Raul should have hooked himself up with her. 'I guess I'm too old for this.'

His dark eyes narrowed on her face. 'You're not old,' he argued. Then, his lips twitching at her tongue-in-cheek expression, 'I mean it. You can't be more than what? Thirty-two, thirty-three? That is not old, believe me.'

Ally gave him an old-fashioned look. 'If that's a sneaky way of getting me to tell you how old I am, you needn't have bothered. I'm not ashamed of my age. I'm thirty-eight; almost thirty-nine, in fact. Comfortably middle-aged.'

He shook his head. 'Why do you persist in putting yourself down?' he exclaimed. 'I wasn't exaggerating. You don't look your age, however much you might like to believe you do.'

'Really?'

'Yes, really.' Raul regarded her with a disturbingly sensual gaze. 'Who told you you were—what was it you said?—comfortably middle-aged? Some man?'

'Isn't it always?' Ally was sardonic. Then, because that was one thing she couldn't blame Jeff for, she added, 'No, actually, it was Sam. My daughter. I think she thought it was a compliment.'

'You have a daughter?' He was polite, but wary, she thought, and she wondered if he was speculating about her husband. 'Well, children can be very—very—'

'Honest?'

'No.' His smile returned. 'I was going to say cruel. And short-sighted. They see what they want to see. How old is—Sam?'

Too late, Ally realised she had told him Sam's real name. 'She's twenty,' she admitted, with some reluctance. And then, because anything she told him was unlikely to go any further, she added. 'She's getting married next year. I think she wants to make me a grandmother.' Her expression grew unknowingly wistful. 'I suppose she assumes I've got nothing else to look forward to.'

Raul shook his head. 'That's some opinion you've got of yourself, isn't it?' He paused before continuing, 'Does your husband agree with her?'

Ally's lips tightened. 'Her father and I are divorced.'

'Ah.'

His response was typical and Ally felt a sudden resurgence of the determination that had got her to buy her ticket to San Cristobál in the first place. 'What do you mean—ah?' she demanded hotly. 'Does the fact that I'm divorced explain everything? Is that what you're thinking? A woman scorned and all that guff? Well, let me tell you, I'm glad to be out of that relationship.'

'If you say so.'

'I do say so.' Ally resented having to defend herself to him. 'And now, if you'll excuse me—'

'Wait!' As she would have slid off her stool, his lean brown fingers closed about her wrist, and her heart pounded wildly through her veins. 'Don't go,' he pleaded, his dark eyes warm and appealing. 'If I've offended you, I'm sorry. That was not my intention.'

'Which begs the question, what was your intention in approaching me?' retorted Ally tersely. And then, becoming aware that their heated exchange was attracting the attention of other people around them, she lowered her tone. 'Please let me go. I have a table booked in the restaurant.'

Raul sighed. 'So do I.'

Ally was not impressed. 'So?'

Raul's thumb pressed insistently against the network of

veins that marked the inner side of her wrist. 'We could have dinner together—'

'I don't think so.'

'Why not?' Despite her obvious opposition, he held on to her arm. 'We're both on our own, aren't we? Why shouldn't we share a table?'

'It doesn't occur to you that I might not want to, does it?' she exclaimed. 'And why should you be so certain that I'm on my own? I could be with—with someone else. Just because I'm divorced—'

'Are you?'

'I told you I was.'

'No, I mean, are you with someone?' he asked softly, and, meeting his disturbing eyes, Ally felt her resistance falter.

'I—could be.'

He conceded the point. 'But are you?'

Ally's breath came out with a resigned gulp. 'No.'

'So?' His thumb softened on her wrist, finding her pulse and massaging its erratic beat with gentle insistence. 'Will you let me buy you dinner?'

Ally shook her head. 'I don't know why you should want to.'

His lips twisted. 'Put it down to my idiosyncrasy,' he said drily. 'Shall we go?'

# CHAPTER TWO

THE restaurant was busy and the head waiter was more than happy to free up one of his smaller tables by seating them together. The table he gave them was against the far wall, with a trellis of ornamental greenery giving an added touch of privacy. Ally wasn't at all sure she appreciated being made to feel as if they were indulging in some kind of squalid assignation, and although she allowed herself to be seated, she couldn't help glancing about her, sure that their unlikely liaison must be the cynosure of all eyes.

But nobody seemed interested in them. The other diners were too busy getting on with their own lives to pay any attention to the two people who were sharing the table that was half hidden by the trellis. Forcing herself to calm down, she smoothed her moist palms over the skirt of her dress.

'Stop looking as if you'd rather be any place than here,' said Raul mildly, after the waiter had placed two folded menus on the table. 'You're beginning to give me a complex.'

Ally pulled a wry face. 'Oh, right.'

'I mean it.' His eyes were amused. 'I have to tell you, I don't usually have to force the women I'm attracted to to endure my company.'

Ally's mouth dried at the unexpected compliment, but she chose not to acknowledge it. 'I bet you don't,' she said, wishing she could be a little more spontaneous. 'Um—I've never been here before.'

'Where? The airport, or this restaurant?'

'This restaurant,' she clarified. 'I have flown out of Heathrow before. We—that is—' She had been about to mention Jeff and she bit her careless tongue with impatience.

14

'As a family,' she amended. 'We've been to the Greek Islands and to Florida.'

'Disneyworld?' he suggested and she smiled.

'Yes. Sam and Ryan loved it.'

He frowned. 'Ryan? That would be your—?'

'My son,' put in Ally quickly. 'Sam and Ryan are twins.'

'I see.' He paused. 'So you have two children?'

'That's right.' Ally caught her lower lip between her teeth. 'So now you know all about me.'

'Hardly,' he murmured, but she couldn't help wondering what he was thinking and whether the knowledge that she had two children somehow diminished her attraction in his eyes.

Which was ridiculous, she chided herself swiftly. No matter what he'd said, she didn't believe he really was attracted to her. He just found her a novelty, that was all. Perhaps this was just his evening to be kind to dogs and fortyish matrons.

The arrival of the wine waiter to ask if they'd like anything to drink gave her a few moments to collect her thoughts, and after he'd departed to get the bottle of wine Raul had ordered, there was the menu to study.

It was difficult to decide what to eat. Despite the fact that the pounds had dropped off her in the last couple of years, she was still acutely conscious of being overweight. In recent weeks her appetite had been practically non-existent and she'd only eaten at all to satisfy Sam's concern about her. In consequence, her eyes were drawn to the vegetarian dishes, and after some consideration she chose asparagus soup and stuffed avocado with Hollandaise sauce.

'Are you a vegetarian?' Raul asked curiously when she was forced to tell him her selection and Ally managed a rueful smile.

'No.'

'But you prefer vegetarian food?'

Ally sighed. 'I'm just not very hungry,' she murmured, putting the menu aside. 'What are you having?'

Raul shrugged. 'Something simple, I guess. Salad followed by a steak sounds good to me.'

Actually, it sounded good to Ally, too, but the thought of all those calories gave her pause. Besides, there was no guarantee that she'd be able to eat anything. She was so nervous about being here in the first place.

The wine was brought, and their individual meals were ordered, and Ally did her best to relax. It was definitely easier with a glass of Chardonnay in her hand, and she decided it was time he answered a few questions for a change.

'You don't live in England, do you?' she ventured, rather daringly, and his long lashes shaded his eyes.

'What makes you say that?'

'Well…' She could hardly mention his tan. That was too personal. 'Your accent,' she exclaimed, with some relief. 'It doesn't sound wholly British to me.'

His teeth were very white against his dark skin. 'You wound me,' he murmured, but his smile revealed he was only teasing her. 'I thought I spoke very good English.'

'You do.' She hurried to reassure him. 'Just sometimes—' She broke off, losing her nerve. 'I'm sorry. It's nothing to do with me.'

'Why not?' His eyes on her mouth brought a return of the panic she had felt earlier. 'I don't mind telling you. My home is almost in the Caribbean and both my father and mother are of Spanish-American descent.'

'Oh.' Ally took a nervous sip of her wine, and then added rather recklessly, 'I'm going to the Caribbean, too. Tomorrow. Well, to Nassau, anyway. I suppose that's not strictly the Caribbean either, is it?'

'Not strictly,' he conceded. 'But near enough.' He paused. 'Are you going on holiday?'

Ally pressed her lips together, wishing she hadn't been quite so outspoken. But it was too late now, so— 'Yes,' she admitted unwillingly. And then, because she felt the need to explain that she wasn't one of those sad people who holiday alone, 'I'm going to stay with friends.'

'In Nassau?'

*No, San Cristobál.*

But Ally didn't contradict him. 'Yes, Nassau,' she lied, looking down into her glass as she spoke in case her eyes betrayed her. 'Have you been there?'

'Oh, yeah.' He was laconic. 'I've been there. I've been all over the Caribbean. My—that is, the company I work for charters sailing craft to travel firms and private individuals. I used to spend holidays crewing on sloops and schooners.'

Ally was intrigued. 'It sounds fun.'

'It was.' He nodded. 'Hard work, too, particularly if we ran into bad weather.'

'Hurricanes, you mean?' Ally's eyes were wide.

'Hardly.' His lips twitched. 'You don't try to outrun a hurricane. But, if the barometer's falling, and you've got a party of inexperienced tourists on board, you make for the nearest landfall.'

'I see.' Ally felt foolish.

'That's not to say we didn't encounter a squall from time to time,' he assured her gently. 'It rains, you know, even in the Caribbean.'

Ally managed a small smile. 'Not a lot, I hope.'

'No.' He shook his head. 'And not usually at this time of year. I guess you'll be glad to leave the cold weather behind.'

'Mmm.' Ally relaxed again, the anticipation of spending the rest of January and most of February in a warmer climate bringing its own excitement. 'I've never been to the Caribbean before.'

'You'll love it,' he told her, as the waiter arrived with their first course. 'Plenty of sunshine, warm seas, and some of the best seafood in the world.'

Ally smiled, picking up her spoon to tackle her soup. 'No place for a vegetarian, then?' she murmured drily.

'No.' His eyes showed his amusement. 'Do you think I'm biased?'

'Why wouldn't you be?'

'Yeah.' He forked up a mouthful of his green salad. 'I have to admit, I'd hate to live anywhere else.'

Ally licked her lips. 'Have you been on holiday in England?' she asked, amazed at the ease with which the words slipped off her tongue. But, what the hell? she thought determinedly. She was never likely to see him again, and he was so easy to talk to.

'Actually, I've been in London on business,' he replied, evidently not offended by her question. 'I came to visit the Boat Show at Earl's Court. Do you know it?'

'Well, I know Earl's Court,' said Ally, crumbling the roll the waiter had left on her plate. 'But I've never been to the Boat Show. I don't live in London, you see. I live in the north of England. That's why I'm spending the night here. It would have been too much of a gamble to risk connecting with my flight in the morning.'

'Ah.' He gave an understanding nod. 'So your holiday's begun a day early.'

'You could say that.' Ally realised she had finished her soup and felt a moment's surprise. Talking to Raul, she had completely forgotten the problems she'd been having with eating and she half wished she'd taken a chance and ordered a steak, after all. She replaced her spoon and took a mouthful of her wine before continuing. 'That was lovely.'

'I'm glad you enjoyed it.'

'Oh, I did.' Ally propped her elbows on the table and rested her chin on her linked hands. Then, feeling quite expansive, she added, 'As a matter of fact, I haven't had much of an appetite lately. Not since—not since—well, all the fuss.'

Raul regarded her thoughtfully. 'The divorce?' he ventured softly, and she found herself nodding her agreement.

'It was so—ugly,' she said, with a shudder, hardly aware that the amount she had drunk was loosening her tongue. 'We had to sell the house, move into a much smaller semi. And because Sam and Ryan are at college, I've had to do most of the organising on my own.'

'Tough.' Raul was sympathetic. 'Why couldn't your—ex-husband lend a hand?'

'Jeff?' Ally grimaced. 'He wasn't there. He left for Canada before the decree nisi. He's always wanted to travel, and if—when—he marries Kelly he'll probably apply for a Canadian passport.'

Raul frowned. 'What does your husband do?'

'Do? As in, for a living?' She pulled a face. 'He's a biology teacher.'

'Biology?'

Raul grinned and suddenly Ally was grinning, too. 'Yes. Ironic, isn't it?' She stifled a laugh. 'You show me yours and I'll show you mine.'

'So this woman you mentioned, she's a teacher, too?'

'Mmm.' Ally bent her head, aware that she was being far too familiar, and tried to tone the conversation down. 'She—er—she came to Jeff's school on one of those exchange schemes. According to him it was love at first sight.'

'You don't believe it?'

'Oh, no.' Ally looked up, her eyes widening. 'I believe it. She's one of those petite blondes that all men seem to find irresistible. Well, men of a certain age anyway.'

'I don't,' said Raul at once, and Ally gave him a retiring look.

'You're not as old as Jeff,' she said. 'Give it time.'

'I don't need to.' Raul studied her face with disturbing intensity. 'I wouldn't leave you for a bleached blonde.'

Ally dimpled. 'How do you know she was a bleached blonde?'

'Aren't they always?' Raul waited until the waiter had removed their plates before continuing, 'Desperate women, who can't get a man of their own so they resort to stealing someone else's.'

'I don't think Jeff put up much opposition,' said Ally wryly, and Raul shrugged.

'More fool him.'

She giggled then. 'You're awfully good for my ego, do you know that?'

'I aim to please.'

'Yes, you do, don't you?' The colour in her cheeks deepened becomingly. 'I wonder why?'

Now it was Raul's turn to pull a face. 'That sounds suspiciously like a criticism,' he remarked drily. 'Has no one told you what an attractive woman you are?'

'Not recently, no,' Ally admitted. 'Who are you? Some kind of guardian angel employed to comfort lonely women?'

'My name's Raul, not Gabriel,' he retorted, refilling her wine glass. 'Believe it or not, this is the first time I've invited a woman I'd never met before to have dinner with me. I know you think I'm stringing you a line, but I'm not. I genuinely am enjoying myself.'

'So'm I.' Ally looked down into her glass, amazed at her own audacity. 'I'm glad you asked me to have dinner with you.'

'Yeah. Me, too,' he conceded, touching his glass to hers. 'Here's to us.'

'To us,' she repeated obediently, wishing they had longer than tonight to get to know one another better, and was aware of him watching her as she sipped her wine.

The main course was just as delicious as the first, although in all honesty Ally was hardly aware of what she was eating. Afterwards, all she remembered was that Raul had offered her a taste of his steak, and the intimacy of sharing his food had extinguished everything else.

She also knew she had never been as relaxed with a man in her life. Not even Jeff, who had usually dominated their conversations with *his* work, *his* problems. Looking back, she was forced to acknowledge that although she had always thought they had a good marriage, it had hardly been a partnership in the real sense of the word. For years, she'd let Jeff make all the decisions and, because she'd seldom objected, he'd begun to believe that she didn't have an opinion of her own.

Still, she could hardly blame him for that...

She declined a dessert and, instead of staying at the table, they went to have their coffee in the adjoining lounge. They were shown to a table in the shade of a palm. There were two comfortable armchairs and a low sofa set around the table and Ally chose the sofa, expecting Raul to take one of the armchairs opposite.

But he didn't.

'You don't mind, do you?' he asked, when his thigh brushed against hers as he seated himself beside her. She managed to get, 'Not at all,' past the sudden constriction in her throat. She was intensely aware of his closeness, however, and of the fact that his weight depressed the cushion beneath her hip.

'I suppose you're staying at the hotel, too,' she said quickly, to distract herself from the powerful length of his legs that he was forced to fold beneath the table, and Raul waited until the waiter had served their coffee before replying.

'Fourth floor,' he told her easily. 'How about you?'

'Oh, I'm staying here—'

'I know that.' The look he gave her assured her that he hadn't been deceived by her attempt at subterfuge. 'Which floor?'

'I—the first, I think.'

'Don't you know?'

Of course she did. And it wasn't the first.

Pretending to be indignant, she exclaimed, 'Naturally I know which floor my room's on.'

Raul's eyes were far too discerning. 'I happen to know the first floor is given over to offices and conference suites,' he remarked levelly. 'If you don't want to tell me where your room is, okay. You don't have to lie about it, Diana.'

Diana!

Ally felt awful. 'I—my name's not *Diana*,' she admitted weakly. 'It's Ally. Ally Sloan.'

'No kidding?'

He didn't sound surprised and she looked at him a little warily. 'You knew?'

'Well, if you were prepared to lie about which floor your room was on—'

'I wasn't lying, exactly.'

'No.' He was sceptical. 'Don't tell me, they're accommodating you in one of the banqueting halls?'

'You don't have to be sarcastic,' she said, hurt by his tone. 'If I were better at this I wouldn't have chosen that floor in the first place.'

'Why would you want to be better at lying to people?' he demanded in a low disturbing voice. 'Have I given you any reason to be suspicious of me?'

'No.' Ally's tongue circled her lips in innocent provocation. 'But I didn't know that when you spoke to me in the bar.'

Raul's eyes darkened. 'And you feel you know me better now?'

Ally swallowed. 'Well—yes.'

His smile troubled her, but before she had had a chance to wonder what it meant, his hand covering hers in her lap drove all other thoughts out of her head. 'I'm glad,' he said, and she was supremely conscious of his knuckles digging into her thigh, causing a wave of heat to dart upwards into her groin. 'You don't have to be afraid of me.'

'I'm not.'

The words came out automatically but she wasn't at all sure she believed them. Something was warning her that he hadn't been completely honest with her either, and while it was easy to put it down to her own over-active imagination, she still found his attention hard to justify. She simply wasn't the type to attract a man like him—a man as *young* as him—and she wasn't sure how he expected her to proceed.

But he was attractive, and the hand holding hers in her lap was strong and masculine. It reminded her that it had been too long since she'd had a man's hands on her body, and she wondered what he would say if she confessed that she'd only ever been to bed with one man in her entire life. She was hopelessly naïve when it came to the way men and women conducted themselves today, and although Sam had done her best to educate her, she'd never expect her mother to find herself in a situation like this.

However, thinking about Sam made her realise how shocked her daughter would be if she could see her now. It was one thing for Sam to expound the sexual advantages women enjoyed today and quite another for her to face the fact that her mother was still a comparatively young woman and might be sexually attracted to some other man. Sam was disgusted with her father's behaviour but that didn't mean she'd forgive her mother's transgressions, even if the circumstances were totally different now.

Tugging her fingers out of Raul's grasp, Ally took refuge in her coffee, almost spilling it when he squeezed her thigh. As he did so, all the bones in her limbs turned to water and a pulse she'd hardly been aware of before beat insistently between her legs. Dear God, she thought, did he know what he was doing to her; had he guessed how emotionally starved she was?

'Would you like another drink?'

To her relief, he removed his hand from her thigh and contented himself with turning sideways to face her. His knee nudged her leg and she had to steel herself not to move away. But perhaps another drink wasn't a bad idea, she thought breathlessly. It might help to calm the nerves jumping in her stomach.

'Why not?' she said, promising herself she'd have one more drink and then say goodnight. She wanted to be up bright and early in the morning. After all the effort Suzanne had made, the least she could do was not to miss the plane.

Raul summoned the waiter and ordered himself a Scotch over ice and Ally another vodka and tonic. Even the drink she'd chosen was a cliché, she thought impatiently. Why couldn't she have ordered a champagne cocktail or a spritzer?

She noticed that Raul had put one arm along the back of the sofa now and she wished she had the nerve to sit back in her seat and see what he would do. As it was, she was perched on the edge of the cushions, her knees pressed tightly together.

The waiter returned with their drinks and Ally picked up her glass and took a reassuring gulp. But she had the feeling it would take more than another drink to make her relax. She was far too tense for relaxation; far too aware of him and the temptation he evinced.

'So what made you decide to go to the Bahamas?' he asked, lifting his own drink to his lips.

'Oh—you know.' Ally shrugged, collecting her thoughts. 'Sam thought it would be a good idea for me to have a holiday.'

'Your daughter?'

'Mmm.' She smiled. 'Like I said, she feels she has to look after me.'

'I'm not surprised.' Raul regarded her gently. 'You have that effect on people.'

'Oh, I don't think—'

'I mean it.' To her consternation, she felt the brush of his fingers against her nape. 'You're very appealing, Ally. It's quite a novelty to meet a woman who is so lacking in self-conceit.'

Ally blushed. She couldn't help it. 'You're just trying to embarrass me now,' she accused him uncomfortably. She picked up her glass again. 'When I've had this, I'm going to have to say goodnight.'

Raul glanced at the narrow gold watch on his wrist. 'It's early yet,' he protested.

'For you, maybe.' Ally caught herself before she admitted that she was usually in bed by half-past ten these days. She glanced behind her. 'I just want to speak to the waiter first.'

'The waiter?'

'In the restaurant,' Ally explained. Then, with a certain amount of reticence, 'I want to ask him to add the cost of my dinner to my room bill, that's all.' She looked round again. 'I wonder where he is?'

'It's dealt with.' Raul took a deep breath as Ally turned confused eyes in his direction. 'I signed the bill before we left the restaurant.'

'Oh, but—'

'I hope you're not going to embarrass me by refusing to let me buy your dinner,' he said mildly. 'It was my pleasure. As I said before, this has been a very pleasant evening.'

'For me, too,' said Ally impulsively, and he tugged on a strand of her hair.

'Then perhaps you'll allow me to escort you to your room?' he suggested, causing her stomach to plunge uncertainly. He grinned. 'I'm sure Sam would approve.'

Ally was equally sure that Sam wouldn't, but she could hardly say that. Not when he had been kind enough to pay for her drinks and her dinner, and for the wine she had consumed so freely throughout the meal. So, 'All right,' she agreed, a little breathily, and forced herself not to flinch when he put a hand in the small of her back as he guided her out of the lounge a few minutes later.

# CHAPTER THREE

IT HAD been a dull overcast morning when they'd left London but Nassau was basking in the heat of the afternoon sun. Ally estimated that the temperature outside the airport buildings was hovering somewhere close to ninety. Heat shimmered above the tarmac of the runways and the breeze that stirred the flags hanging limply from their poles was barely enough to temper the humidity that drifted into the Arrivals Hall.

She and her fellow passengers were waiting for their luggage to be unloaded onto the carousels, and, exchanging a rueful smile with a young mother who was trying to appease two fretful children, Ally tried to rekindle the optimism she'd felt when she'd left Newcastle the afternoon before. She was almost there, she thought determinedly. According to Suzanne, it was just a short flight from New Providence to San Cristobál, where her friend and her husband ran a small hotel. Suzanne had said someone would meet her here at the airport and escort her to the small plane that would take her on the final leg of her journey, and, apart from her own foolish feelings, everything was going according to plan.

Only it wasn't, Ally reflected unhappily. Nothing had gone according to plan since she'd allowed Raul—if that really was his name—to pick her up in the hotel bar the night before. Ever since then everything had gone anything but according to plan and she was having a hard time fighting the suspicion that perhaps this holiday wasn't such a good idea, after all.

Which was defeatist, perhaps, but it was how she felt. Last night she'd done something totally reckless, totally irresponsible, and all she'd really wanted to do this morning was get on the train again and go home. She wasn't the kind of woman who could do what she'd done and not get a conscience about it. She'd acted completely out of character, and she dreaded to think how her daughter would feel if she ever found out.

Of course, there was no reason why Sam should find out, she assured herself. No matter how much she'd wanted to do it, she hadn't cashed in her air ticket or cancelled her trip, and surely by the time she got back she'd have forgotten all about last night. She doubted if Suzanne would blame her, if she confided in her, but then Suzanne was a woman of the world whereas, for all her modern outlook, Sam could be incredibly old-fashioned when it came to the people she loved.

'Mrs Sloan?'

The voice came from behind her and when she turned Ally found a man in a short-sleeved shirt and khaki shorts gazing cheerfully at her. He was very tanned, with a fan of creases at each side of his blue eyes that seemed to indicate he spent a lot of time outdoors. Grey-blond hair escaped untidily from the sides of the baseball cap he was wearing back to front and his smile revealed white, but slightly crooked, teeth.

'Yes, I'm Mrs Sloan,' she said, and he nodded.

'I thought you must be.' His grin deepened. 'Suze said to look out for a tall good-looking woman and she wasn't wrong.' He pulled off his cap and held out his hand. 'Mike Mclean at your service, Mrs Sloan. I'm here to fly you over to Saint Chris.'

'Saint Chris?'

Ally arched an enquiring brow and he gestured towards the carousel. 'San Cristobál,' he explained. 'D'you want to point out your bags and we'll be on our way?'

'My bags?' Ally turned back to the conveyor belt that was now moving. 'Oh—yes.' She shook her head a little dazedly. 'I thought—that is, I assumed that whoever Suzanne had sent would be waiting outside.'

'In this heat?' Mclean grimaced. 'No. So long as we go through Customs together no one objects.' He saw her move forward. 'That's one of them?'

In a short while, Mclean had the sports holdall she had borrowed from Ryan and her own suitcase on a luggage trolley and was propelling them towards the exit. Although he wasn't a particularly tall man, he was obviously strong and capable, and Ally felt no qualms about putting herself into his hands. Indeed, it was a relief to be free of the responsibility for getting to her destination, and she fanned herself a little weakly when they emerged into the sunlight.

'It's this way,' he said, directing her along the walkway that led towards the commuter terminal. 'Did you have a good journey?'

'Um—fairly good.' Ally was loath to tell him that she'd slept most of the way. But she'd been exhausted and, after lunch had been served, she'd flaked out.

'Marvellous things, these big jets,' commented Mclean amiably. 'Makes my little Piper look like a kid's toy.' He grinned again. 'I guess you'd know about kids. Suze tells me you've got two of your own.'

'They're hardly kids,' murmured Ally. She paused. 'Do you have children, Mr Mclean?'

'The name's Mike,' he said at once. 'And, no. I'm afraid I've never had that pleasure. I'm what Suze calls a crusty old bachelor. More's the pity.'

Ally smiled. 'Hardly crusty,' she said. 'And please call me Ally. Mrs Sloan makes me sound like my mother-in-law. My ex-mother-in-law, I mean,' she added hastily. 'I'm divorced.'

'Yeah. Suze told me that, too,' he admitted, his tone sympathetic. Then, 'But you've done the right thing coming out here. Smuggler's Cove is a beautiful spot.'

'Is it?' Smuggler's Cove was where Suzanne and her husband, Peter Davis, had their hotel. 'I'm looking forward to seeing it. To seeing the whole island,' she appended. 'Is it very big?'

'Nah. About eight miles long and five across at best.' He saw she was flagging and waited for her to catch up. 'Of course, Suze will have told you that the Ramirezes own most of the island, but what's left is pretty damn spectacular, I can tell you.'

Ally frowned. 'Why would Suzanne have mentioned— who was it you said?—the Ramirezes to me?'

'Well, because Julia is going to marry their son,' explained Mike carelessly. Julia was Suzanne's daughter, Ally recalled. He pointed at the single-engined aircraft that awaited them on the tarmac. 'There's my pride and joy. And don't worry; I've got an icebox on board. I bet you could murder a cold drink?'

He hastened ahead so that by the time she'd reached the small Cherokee he'd already stowed her bags in the back. 'Welcome aboard,' he said, helping her up the short flight of steps into the cabin. 'You're going to feel a whole lot better when we get off the ground.'

Ally hoped so. Right now, she felt hot and uncomfortable, the shirt and denim trousers that had felt too thin in London now damp and sticking to her skin. She'd removed the jacket she'd worn to travel in as soon as she'd got off the plane but she was still sweating. She should have brought a change of clothes in her hand luggage, she thought ruefully. But then, this morning she'd been too bemused to think of things like that.

This morning…

Pushing that thought aside, she settled into the seat beside Mike and sipped a cola as he completed his pre-flight checks. Then he adjusted his earphones and she heard the static buzz as the control tower responded to his request for clearance for take-off.

'Not long now,' he said, covering the mouthpiece with his hand. 'These guys are pretty efficient.'

Ally nodded, hoping she wouldn't disgrace herself. She'd never flown in such a small aircraft before and, when Mike taxied to the end of the runway, she felt her stomach quiver.

But then they were moving, faster and faster, and in no time at all it seemed they were off the ground and soaring into the blue, blue sky. Nassau, and the island of New Providence, fell away below them and although she still felt a little nervous, her fears seemed foolish. Mike was obviously at home behind the controls and his enthusiasm was infectious.

'Is that San Cristobál?' she asked, after a few minutes, noticing another island on the horizon. But Mike shook his head.

'Hell, no,' he exclaimed. 'That's Andros. It's the biggest island in the group. San Cristobál is one of the smallest.'

'Oh.'

Ally grimaced and Mike grinned at her. 'Hey, it was a reasonable question,' he said. Then, pointing down, he added, 'Can you see the reef? It runs the whole length of Andros. People come from all over the world to dive around the coral.'

'Really?'

Ally gazed down, entranced, and forgot to be worried. There was so much more to see from this small plane than from the big jumbo that she'd flown in from London. She could see dozens of islands now, strung out like pearls across the ocean, and even the sails of larger yachts that were cruising the calm waters below them.

Her stomach tightened. Perhaps one of those yachts was owned by the company Raul worked for, she thought tensely. He'd said they chartered yachts all over the Caribbean, catering to the increasingly popular demand for sailing craft. She wished she'd asked him what the name of the company was. Although he probably wouldn't have told her. A man who slept with a woman and then left before she woke up was hardly likely to leave his calling card.

She pressed her lips together. It was her own fault, of course. There was no point in blaming him for what had happened. It was she who'd let him buy her a drink; she who'd accepted his invitation to dinner. And it was she who'd invited him into her room for a nightcap, precipitating the events that had followed...

She shivered. It all seemed faintly unbelievable now, but it had happened. She had done all those things and more besides. If she was now regretting the whole affair, it served her right. She should have known better.

But, oh, nothing like that had ever happened to her before. All right, she'd been a fool, but she'd also been incredibly vulnerable. Had he guessed that she would have little defence against his practised charm? That, even though he was considerably younger than she was, she wasn't more experienced? It wasn't as if she'd led him on. Or not intentionally, she amended, with a grimace.

And yet, had it been such a bad experience? Ally sighed. If she was absolutely honest with herself she would have to admit that it hadn't. In fact, it was probably because it had been so incredibly satisfying that she was feeling so hurt—so confused—now.

But what had she expected? That something more would come of it? That he might swear undying love for her on the basis of one good night's sex? Come on, Ally, she chided herself inwardly. Grow up!

But she couldn't prevent her mind from drifting back to the moment when they'd reached her door and the mistake she'd made by inviting him in...

'I—want to thank you again,' she began, fumbling in her bag for her key-card. 'You've saved me from spending a rather anxious evening on my own. I'm not used to travelling alone, and I was feeling a little apprehensive.'

'My pleasure,' said Raul, taking the rescued key-card out of her hand and inserting it in the lock for her. The green light flashed and he smiled. 'There you go.'

'Thank you.' Ally turned the handle and opened the door. She stepped inside and then glanced back over her shoulder. 'Um—goodnight.'

'Didn't you forget something?'

Ally swallowed. Of course, she thought unhappily. He expected her to invite him in. That was why he'd offered to escort her to her door. All the rooms had mini-bars and he would know that. What could be more natural than to invite him in for a nightcap? It was the accepted thing to do. Or it would be if she had more confidence in herself.

And yet...

'I'm sorry,' she said, not looking at him, pretending to be intent on closing her handbag. 'Er—I should have asked. Would you like to come in for a drink?'

Let him say no, she begged, forcing herself to turn and face him. And then her cheeks burned when she saw the key-card in his hand.

'A drink?' he echoed now, handing her the key-card, and she realised it hadn't been his intention to invade her privacy. 'Well, I—'

'You don't have to if you don't want to,' she broke in hurriedly, but she knew as soon as she spoke that she'd said the wrong thing. She sounded as if she might take offence if he refused, and, as if to endorse this thought, Raul inclined his head.

'Why not?' he said, stretching out an arm to press the door wider. His lips twisted. 'We might as well end the evening as we began it. Please, go ahead.'

A maid had been into the room while she was at dinner and now the queen-size bed was turned down and a cellophane-wrapped chocolate had been placed on her pillow. In the lamplight, the room looked warm and personal and Ally's tension increased in direct opposition to its implied intimacy.

The door closed behind her guest and, casting him a rather panic-stricken glance, she threw her handbag onto the bed and hastened towards the refrigerated cabinet. The cool air from inside was balm to her hot cheeks and she scanned its contents with anxious eyes, looking for a small bottle of single malt.

'Whisky?' she asked, finding what she was looking for and lifting it out. She closed the door of the cabinet with her hip and leaned back against it. 'I'm afraid there doesn't appear to be any ice.'

Raul had paused in the middle of the floor and was looking about him with some interest. But now he regarded her with considering eyes.

'It doesn't matter,' he said. 'In all honesty, I've probably drunk more than I should have anyway.' He gave her a gentle smile. 'But thanks for the offer.'

Ally shook her head. Conversely, now that he was rejecting the drink, she was disappointed. 'Are you sure?' she asked. 'It's no trouble, you know.'

Raul hesitated. 'Well, if you insist…'

'I'll get a glass,' she said, once again on the defensive. 'If you'll excuse me.'

There were glasses in the bathroom, she remembered with some relief, but she had to pass him to get to the bathroom door. Easing round him, she managed to reach her objective without embarrassing herself still further and she gratefully switched on the light. The fluorescent glow was reassuringly bright and she managed to unscrew the cap and pour the contents of the bottle into one of the squat water glasses without spilling any.

She was reluctant to leave the impersonal brilliance of the bathroom for the discreetly lit surroundings of the bedroom, however. Pausing in the doorway, she said, 'Here you are,' and extended the glass towards him so that Raul was obliged to move into the harsher light to take it. She injected a note of polite interest into her voice. 'I hope it's all right.'

'I'm sure it will be.' Raul swallowed a mouthful of the whisky and nodded. 'It's fine,' he said quietly. Then, 'Are you all right?'

'Why wouldn't I be?' Ally wrapped her arms about her midriff. 'Oh—you mean because I'm not having a drink? Well, actually, I feel as though I've drunk too much, too. Particularly as I've got a long flight in the morning. I just hope I'll wake up in time. Perhaps I should order one of those wake-up calls—'

She was babbling; she knew it. And she was hardly surprised when he broke into her prattle to say in an oddly flat tone, 'I'd better go.' He paused. 'I can see I'm making you nervous, and it is late.'

'Oh, but—' Ally moistened her lips. 'You—you haven't finished your drink.'

'It doesn't matter—'

'It does.' Ally gazed at him with wide uncertain eyes, and Raul uttered a groan.

'Don't,' he said. 'Don't look at me like that.' He started towards the door. 'Get a good night's rest.'

'Wait!' Ally went after him. 'I didn't mean—that is, I'm sorry if I've spoiled the evening.'

'You haven't.' He almost growled the words. Then he gave her a tormented look. 'Let me go, Ally Sloan, or I may do something we'll both regret.' His hand came out almost of its own volition and shaped her cheek. 'You're very sweet, do you know that? And I'm old enough to know better.'

Ally drew a trembling breath. 'You're not implying that I invited you in here to—to—'

'I'm not implying anything,' he said huskily. And then, with a muffled oath, he bent his head and brushed her mouth with his...

\*    \*    \*

'If you look there, you can just see San Cristobál.' Mike Mclean's voice dragged her back to the present and she gathered her scattered senses to look where he was pointing. 'Can you see it? It's that fish-tailed island just west of Marlin Cay.'

Ally had no idea what Marlin Cay was, but she recognised San Cristobál from his description. 'Oh, yes,' she said, trying to sound enthusiastic. 'How much longer is it going to take?'

'Oh—ten, fifteen minutes,' replied Mike, giving her a cheerful grin. 'I bet you're looking forward to seeing Suze again. She said you've known one another a long time.'

'That's right.' Ally endeavoured to distract herself from her thoughts.

'How come you haven't been out to see her before?'

'Well…' Ally hesitated. 'It hasn't been—possible.'

She neglected to tell him that both Suzanne and Peter had never liked Jeff; that they'd both thought he was a user and that they thought he'd neglected Ally shamefully in the past. Of course, she'd always defended him in those days. If only she'd known…

'I get you.' She suspected Mike thought that the airfare had proved prohibitive before this. 'Well, I'm sure you're going to have a great time. And any time you need a guide, I want you to know you can count on me.'

Ally smiled. 'You're very kind.'

'Not kind.' Mike winked. 'Just taking advantage of the situation. If I know Suze, she'll have you fixed up with an escort before you know it. I'm staking my claim, that's all.'

Ally's smile thinned a little. She didn't want Suzanne or anyone else 'fixing her up with an escort'. She didn't want an escort. After last night she thought it would be a long time before she allowed any other man to get even half as close to her. God, how had it happened? How could she have been so naïve?

Her skin prickled with the remembrance of how she'd felt

when Raul kissed her. A tingling sensation had begun when his mouth had touched hers and spread throughout her whole body. For a few seconds she'd been unable to move, unable to speak. Unable to do anything, in fact, but absorb the incredulous realisation that he was holding her firmly between his hands and nibbling on her lips.

She took a deep breath. She should have stopped him; she knew that now, had known it then, only she'd been so shocked by the feelings he had so effortlessly inspired that she'd numbed her mind to any kind of mutiny. She'd wanted him to go on; she'd wanted him to kiss her; she'd wanted him to thrust his caressing tongue into her mouth and take possession of her spinning senses.

God, she'd been so easy, she agonised bleakly. She'd always despised women who made fools of themselves over younger men, but she was no better. Yet she'd always considered herself beyond such things. Even when Jeff had left her for a much younger woman, she'd felt a certain amount of scorn for what she'd seen as his attempt to recapture his youth. She would never have dreamed that she could be caught in the same trap, would never have believed she could act that way herself.

So why had she?

As Mike contacted the airport at San Cristobál to negotiate their approach and landing, Ally struggled to understand what Raul had done to make her forsake the woman she'd thought she was and become some wild creature governed by her needs and her emotions.

She pressed her lips tightly together. She couldn't pretend she hadn't known what she was doing. No matter how much easier it would have been for her to blame him for what had happened, she couldn't do it. She'd gone into his arms eagerly, blindly, seeking a crazy gratification that she'd instinctively known that only he could provide.

God, what must he have thought of her? When he'd kissed her, when he'd tilted her chin and looked into her eyes, what had he seen? A timid frightened woman who was suddenly at the mercy of her senses, or a sex-starved harlot with no shame and fewer morals?

She shook her head. Whatever he'd thought, she'd been too bemused to do anything but drown in the sultry heat of his lovemaking. Weak and feeble as the memory was, she'd been trembling with need and emotion, and lost to any will but his.

She seemed to remember he'd said something about this not being supposed to happen, almost as if everything that had happened up to that point had been preordained. But with his thumb tugging at the corner of her lips, she hadn't attempted to ask him what he meant and he hadn't repeated it. His mouth had been too intent on tracing a sensuous path down the curve of her neck while he whispered her name over and over with an almost desperate urgency.

Perhaps that was why she hadn't attempted to stop him, she consoled herself. Perhaps the knowledge that this attractive man was apparently as drunk with his emotions as she was with hers had prevented her from drawing back. But that was wishful thinking. She'd have let him do anything at that moment.

For a second, she felt the quivering in her thighs that she'd felt then, the melting sensation of her bones dissolving, of her legs becoming like jelly beneath her. His hands had caressed her throat, she remembered, sliding beneath the neckline of her dress, exposing the pale skin of her shoulders. For the first time in her life she'd been glad that there was flesh on her bones and that she didn't have the saltcellar hollows that young women seemed to think was such an essential to beauty today.

She'd hardly been aware that he'd found the zip at the back of her dress until it slid away to pool in a circle of black silk about her ankles. But the amazing thing was that she hadn't been embarrassed standing there in little more than her bra and pantyhose while he was still fully clothed.

But that didn't stop her from cringing now. God, she must have been drunk—and not just on her emotions. She could think of no other reason why she would have acted so out of character. She was simply not that kind of woman. Until now, she'd lived a perfectly decent life. Having sex with a stranger she'd only met hours before was the stuff of romantic novels; not real life. Yet when he'd touched her, when he'd pulled her against his lean, muscled body and tantalised her with his teasing mouth, she'd felt as if she had no will of her own.

How had it happened? When his lips had returned to hers with what had felt suspiciously like hunger, why had she wound her arms around his neck and given him back kiss for kiss? Dear Lord, she'd behaved as if she was greedy for his lovemaking, raising herself up on her toes, revelling in the hard strength she could feel between his thighs, fitting her quivering body to his.

For his part Raul had offered no opposition. On the contrary, for some reason he'd seemed to find her—what? Her inexperience? Her naïvety? Her *desperation*? She shuddered—exciting. He'd been so different from Jeff, she conceded tensely, taking her with him every step of the way. She couldn't even pretend that she'd thought of her ex-husband when she was in Raul's arms. There had been no comparison between Jeff's solid frame and Raul's sinuous masculinity; no similarity whatsoever in their approach.

The truth was Jeff had never made love to her with even half of the skill that Raul had so carelessly exhibited, and even with her eyes closed she could not have mistaken his identity. She had never experienced such power, such tenderness, such suppressed passion, that had been at once flattering and thrilling. And, oh, so unbelievably good.

Half afraid that Mike would notice the way she was twisting her hands together in her lap, she turned her head to stare out of the plane's window. They'd be landing soon, she reminded herself. She had to stop thinking about what had happened last night and start anticipating her arrival. She had weeks ahead of her to relax and do whatever she wanted, and surely now that she'd got Jeff out of her system she was not going to make the mistake of letting one unguarded incident ruin her holiday.

All the same, images of herself and Raul together refused to be banished. They had done things that she and Jeff had never done, not even when they were first married. But then, he'd seduced her before she was old enough to know better and, with the twins on the way, she'd been pathetically eager to accept his proposal.

She sighed.

Nevertheless, nothing could excuse the way she'd behaved last night. She hadn't gone to bed with Raul because she'd felt some latent desire to prove herself. She'd slept with him because she'd wanted to, because she'd wanted to please him—and that was the saddest thing of all.

Still caught up in the spell of emotions she'd never felt before, she'd spared little thought for what was right or wrong. When Raul had tossed his jacket aside and torn off his tie, she'd shocked herself by reaching for the buttons of his shirt. She'd been frantic for him to take his clothes off, frantic to touch him, and when she'd spread her palms against his taut midriff, she'd been almost dizzy with longing.

And Raul hadn't given her time to have any doubts. His tongue had painted a sensuous path from her jawline to the rising swell of her breasts, drawing her bra away from her burgeoning nipples before suckling on their tender tips. As if compelled, his mouth had returned to hers again and again and there'd been a sensual pleasure in feeling the abrasion of his chest hair against her sensitive skin.

Somehow, she didn't altogether remember how it had happened, they'd been on the bed and she'd been helping him kick off his boots and trousers. He'd been wearing black satin boxers, she recalled tremulously, and they hadn't been able to hide the impressive bulge of his erection.

She trembled now, remembering it was she who'd peeled his shorts away and exposed his sex to her intoxicated gaze. *Intoxicated!* Her lips twisted. She'd been intoxicated all right. Intoxicated in more ways than one.

But had he been intoxicated, too? It had certainly seemed so at the time though she couldn't help wondering now if he hadn't known exactly what he was doing. She could still see him caressing her inner thighs, tucking his thumbs into the hem of her briefs and tugging them off.

After that they'd both seemed to go a little crazy. She stifled a groan. When had she become the sort of woman who opened herself to a man's lips and his tongue, who let a man seduce her in ways she'd only read about before? Had she really spread her legs and arched against his tormenting caresses, welcomed the thrust of his tongue that had driven her to the very edge of insanity? And had she sighed with satisfaction when he'd sheathed his rampant shaft in the moist heart of her womanhood, wrapped her legs about his waist and urged him to go on?

She knew she had; knew, too, that she'd been pitifully eager for him to take possession of her, encouraging him with breathless little sounds that even then she'd hardly recognised as issuing from her mouth. She'd been deaf and blind to everything but the things he was doing to her and when her climax had come she remembered he'd silenced her grateful cry with his lips.

Her tongue circled her teeth. Thank God he'd had the sense to wear protection, she acknowledged unsteadily. If he hadn't she might have been facing something much worse than losing her self-respect. How convenient that he'd found the contraceptive in his pocket, she thought bitterly, wondering if a man ever suffered the same regrets as a woman. Probably not, she decided wryly. He hadn't confessed to her that he'd never felt like that before…

# CHAPTER FOUR

THE plane banked suddenly and Ally clutched her seat, drawing a sympathetic grin from her companion. 'Sorry about that,' he apologised. 'But we'll be landing in a couple of minutes and there was no easy way to wake you.'

Ally stared at him. 'I wasn't asleep.'

'No?' He smirked. 'Well, you had your eyes closed anyway. Don't worry. I won't tell anyone.'

Ally decided not to argue with him. It was probably better if he thought she'd been dozing rather than reliving one of the most humiliating experiences of her life. 'Thanks,' she said, managing a dry tone. 'I suppose I am tired. I was—up—very early this morning.'

Only to discover Raul was gone, she recalled unwillingly. Foolishly perhaps, she'd expected him to be there, but she knew now that that had been unrealistic. And yet, after he had spent more than half the night making mad passionate love to her, she had hoped he might have something more to say to her. Even if it was just goodbye.

But she'd been wrong. He'd evidently made his escape while she was still sleeping and she'd been left with a hollow sense of abandonment. And yet, what had she expected? Everything that needed to be said had been said the night before, and he'd certainly saved them both the embarrassment of making small talk this morning.

All the same, she couldn't help wondering where he'd gone. She'd even entertained the idea that he might have been flying home with the same airline she was using, but, although she'd faced that possibility with a certain amount of trepidation, there'd been no sign of him at the departure gate.

42

Pushing these thoughts aside, she determinedly turned her attention to her present surroundings. There was a runway below them now, a narrow strip of asphalt with a belt of greenery on one side and a sandy shoreline on the other. A beach the colour of bleached bones sloped towards the blue-green waters that lapped its sands, a lacy edging of foam advancing and receding with the incoming tide.

Ally was so entranced with the view that she barely noticed the touch-down, only becoming aware that they had landed when Mike applied the air brakes. 'Welcome to San Cristobál,' he said, easing the aircraft off the runway and into one of the holding bays. 'I know you're going to love being here.'

'I hope so.' Ally gazed about her with bemused eyes. 'It's so beautiful. I can hardly believe I'm here at last.'

'You'll get used to it,' said Mike drily, taxi-ing towards a handful of colour-washed buildings with corrugated iron roofs. He nodded towards a group of people gathered around a cream convertible and a pink buggy. 'Looks like you've got a welcoming committee. That's Suze's buggy and the coupé belongs to Finisterre. I guess young Ramirez must be expected back today, too.'

Ally turned to look at him. 'Finisterre?' she said, looking puzzled.

'Yeah, Finisterre.' Mike grinned as he brought the small aircraft to a halt. 'That's the name Rodrigo Ramirez gave his estate—oh, it must be over a hundred years ago now. Rodrigo, by all accounts, was a bit of a villain. Didn't mind turning his hand to anything so long as it made money.'

Ally's eyebrows lifted. 'Smuggling, you mean?'

'Among other things,' said Mike wryly. 'Here comes Suze. Let me get the door open.'

Taking off his headphones, he stood and climbed over the console into the rear of the plane. Releasing her safety belt, Ally did likewise, fanning herself with the empty cola can

when a draught of hot air from the opening door engulfed
her.

'Ally!' Suzanne was waiting impatiently at the bottom of
the steps that Mike had lowered. 'Oh, Ally, hurry up and
get down here. I want to give you a hug.'

Ally felt the unaccustomed prick of tears as her friend
enfolded her in her arms. At least Suzanne hadn't changed,
she thought gratefully. She was just as warm and exuberant
as she remembered, if a little unfamiliar in her sleeveless
vest and cotton shorts. And so brown, mused Ally enviously,
drawing back to look at her. Even her dark hair had been
striped in shades of gold and copper so that she looked both
casual and sophisticated.

'It's so good to see you again,' Suzanne added, before
Ally could say anything. 'It must be six years since I was
last in England.'

'Seven,' said Ally, smiling though her tears. 'Oh,
Suzanne, I've missed you.'

'Me, too,' said Suzanne, turning to the young woman who
had come to join them. 'Julia, you remember my friend Ally,
don't you?'

'Oh, sure.'

Julia smiled a welcome, but she was shading her eyes and
watching the horizon as her mother spoke, and Suzanne
pulled a face.

'Don't mind her,' she said. 'Her boyfriend's due back
from England today, too. I did tell you Julia was planning
on getting married, didn't I?'

'Well—'

Ally started to explain that Mike Mclean had mentioned
something about it, but Suzanne didn't wait for an answer,
'You didn't meet him, did you? I told him to look out for
you at the airport, but I suppose it was unrealistic to expect
him to pick you out of the crowd.'

'I—' Ally shook her head. 'No, I—I don't think so.' But

had she? A feeling of apprehension swept over her. 'What—what's his name?'

'There it is!'

Julia's sudden cry caused everyone to look skyward and Suzanne gave her daughter's shoulder a comforting squeeze. 'I knew he wouldn't be long,' she said. And then, to Ally, 'Julia and Carlos—that's the Ramirezes' younger son—have been here for over half an hour waiting for the plane. He's been away for ten days, so, as you can imagine, Julia's pretty eager to have him back again.'

'Yes?' Ally swallowed, noticing that Julia gave her mother an impatient look. 'You didn't tell me what his name was—'

'I'll give you a hand with the luggage, shall I?' Mike, who had unloaded Ally's bags as she and Suzanne were greeting one another, now intervened. 'You want them in the buggy, right, Suze?'

'Oh, there's no need for you to do that,' protested Ally, and Suzanne echoed her sentiments.

Summoning one of the porters who had been standing beside the convertible talking to an olive-skinned young man who Ally presumed was Julia's future brother-in-law, she added, 'Thanks, Mike. I really do appreciate this.'

'And me,' put in Ally quickly. 'It was a lovely flight.'

'Well, I'm sure you'll have the chance to thank him again,' remarked Suzanne smugly. 'Mike's going to come and have supper with us one evening while you're here, aren't you, darling?'

'It'll be my pleasure,' said Mike, and, intercepting the glance he exchanged with her friend, Ally couldn't help remembering what he'd said about Suzanne's propensity for matchmaking. Ally hoped she wasn't going to have to hurt anyone's feelings in the days ahead.

The sunlight glinting on the silver paintwork of the plane that was presently making its approach to the island reminded her that it might hold a more immediate danger, however. For a moment, her eyes were glued to the sleek craft and her mouth dried at the prospect of being proved right. But it couldn't be true, she told herself. The man she'd met so briefly and known so intimately couldn't be Suzanne's future son-in-law. Life couldn't be that cruel.

'We'll leave them to it, shall we?' Suzanne's hand tucked comfortingly into her arm distracted her attention. 'You'll meet him soon enough. Tomorrow, probably. We've all been invited to supper at Finisterre. That's the Ramirezes' estate. It's at the other end of the island.'

Ally allowed herself to be drawn towards the pink buggy. The other porters who'd been talking to Carlos Ramirez smiled as she climbed into the buggy beside Suzanne. Carlos, himself, was more intent on the approaching aircraft, but he gave both women a casual wave.

'They're such friendly people,' said Suzanne, albeit a little patronisingly, waving away the dollar notes that Ally wanted her to offer to the porter. 'I've taken care of it,' she insisted, starting the buggy's engine. 'Just relax and enjoy the ride.'

With a careless farewell to her daughter, Suzanne drove through the cluster of palms that backed onto the airport buildings, emerging onto a narrow tarmacked road. Thankfully, the buggy had a canopy to protect its passengers and the breeze caused by the passage of the vehicle through the air helped to cool Ally's burning cheeks.

Trying to stop thinking about the man they were waiting for at the airport, she looked purposefully about her. There was colour everywhere: in the shadowed hills that rose above the coastal belt and in the transparent movement of the ocean. Flowering plants and shrubs were common, it seemed, with pastel-coloured clapboard houses hiding amongst the trees. Ally saw a lizard scampering up the trunk of what she thought was a fig tree, its green scales disappearing into the foliage. She could even hear the faint rhythm of a steel band, but when she mentioned it to Suzanne, her friend explained that what she could probably hear was someone playing their boom box too loud.

'You'll get used to it,' she said, slowing as they rounded a bend in the road and found an ox-cart labouring ahead of them. 'Bahamians love music, particularly beat music. It's an integral part of their lives.'

Ally sighed. 'And you still love it out here, obviously.' She paused. 'I envied you, you know. Leaving England; starting afresh.'

'Well, there was nothing stopping you and Jeff from doing the same,' pointed out Suzanne practically. 'I mean, Jeff being a teacher and all. Teachers are always in demand.'

Ally gave a wry smile. 'I suppose that's why he's gone to work in Canada,' she said.

'Oh, Ally!' Suzanne cast her friend a rueful look. 'I'm sorry. That was tactless. Still, it's probably better if we get it out of the way straight off, don't you think?'

Ally shrugged. 'I suppose so.'

But she sounded a little doubtful and Suzanne stared impatiently at her. 'You're not still in love with him, are you?' she exclaimed. 'For God's sake, Ally, it's been almost two years! You can't be hoping he might come back?'

'I'm not.'

Ally was relieved to find she meant it. After what had happened last night, she was finding it incredibly difficult to even remember what Jeff looked like, let alone anything else. But she couldn't tell Suzanne that; couldn't tell her anything if what she half suspected was true. Not that it was, she assured herself firmly. She was just feeling guilty because of the way things had turned out.

'Well, I'm glad to hear it,' Suzanne declared now. 'I want you to regard this holiday as a new start. At least you and Jeff never came here together, so it has no bad associations. And I know Pete's looking forward to your visit. We've both wanted to show you the hotel for so long.'

'I know.' Ally took a deep breath. 'And I've wanted to

come here. I'm really looking forward to this holiday. As you say, it's exactly what I need.'

Suzanne looked pleased, but they were approaching the outskirts of a small town and for a while she had to concentrate on her driving. Other vehicles, carts and bicycles as well as a number of cars and mini-buses, clogged the narrow streets, and pedestrians showed little concern for their safety.

'This is San Cristobál town,' Suzanne explained, when she got the chance, blowing her horn at an elderly Chrysler saloon that had just lumbered into her path. 'Honestly,' she fumed, 'driving here is becoming impossible.' She pressed her horn again and leaned over her door to remonstrate with the driver. 'Look where you're going, can't you? And get that rattletrap out of my way!'

Ally had to smile at her friend's frustration. She'd forgotten how short-tempered Suzanne could be. But it was difficult negotiating between stalls piled high with fruit and vegetables, and the pungent scent of seafood was very strong.

'It's not much further, thank goodness,' Suzanne said, after steering round the obstacles. 'It's market day and people come into town from all over the island to shop. It's not usually so busy. But there are quite a few shops selling clothes and souvenirs. We get our share of tourists on the island, though I have to say that most people are employed by the Ramirezes in one capacity or another.'

Ally took a deep breath, deciding it was now or never. 'Um—you never did tell me what Julia's boyfriend is called.'

'Oh—Rafael,' said Suzanne at once. 'Rafael Ramirez, of course. You'll like him, Ally. He's a darling. He and Julia have known one another for years.'

Ally expelled the breath she'd been holding. 'Rafael?' she said faintly. 'What an unusual name.'

'Mmm.' Suzanne was reflective. 'Not that anyone except his parents calls him anything but Raul these days.'

*     *     *

Ally stood on her balcony gazing out at the view. The room she'd been allocated overlooked the sandy cove that gave the hotel its name. Beyond the balcony, a stretch of sun-dried turf gave onto a sandy bluff that appeared to fall away rather sharply to the beach below. To the west of the cove, a rocky outcrop provided a natural barrier, while to the south the land curved round as she'd seen from the air, sheltering the cove from the ocean. It was the perfect spot for bathing and Ally assured herself that she'd spend many hours improving her swimming skills in those calm waters.

If she ever got up the courage to leave her room, of course, she reminded herself grimly. God, she couldn't believe how unlucky she'd been. After last night, she'd been sure that nothing worse could happen to her, but she'd been wrong. Of all the men she might have met, why had she had the misfortune to encounter Raul Ramirez? It had to be him. She had no doubts on that score. What troubled her most was why he'd singled her out for his attentions.

She sighed, turning her back on the view and resting her hips on the wrought-iron handrail. She didn't delude herself by thinking that it was her appearance that had attracted him. Apart from anything else, there was the age difference, and the fact that she'd been suspicious of him from the start. Unless he got his kicks from seducing immature older women. Perhaps he'd felt sorry for her. She'd been so obviously out of her depth.

Unless... She frowned. Suzanne had said that she'd asked him to look out for her. But that had been at the airport, not at the airport hotel. And besides, she'd told him her name was Diana. Or she had to begin with. When he'd invited her to have dinner with him, he could have had no idea who she was.

But later... Her cheeks suffused with colour. He had known who she was then. She'd told him. So that meant that when he'd gone to bed with her, he'd known exactly who she was.

Which made it all so much worse, so much more sordid. How could he have done it? How could he have slept with her knowing full well that she was going to stay with his girlfriend's parents? God, it just got worse and worse. What was she going to do?

Leaving the balcony, she walked into the bedroom, looking about her with hot, tear-filled eyes. It was such a lovely room, with light pine furniture and a gaily patterned bedspread that matched the long curtains at the French windows. A jug of purple lilies stood on a bureau, looking suitably exotic, and in the adjoining bathroom there was a basket filled with shampoos and conditioners and all manner of cosmetic aids to beauty.

Suzanne and her husband had gone out of their way to make her feel at home, she thought unhappily. They obviously wanted her to feel loved and pampered and they'd given her one of the best rooms in the hotel. At present, she was supposed to be spoiling herself with a lazy bath and resting for a couple of hours before the evening meal. But how could she relax here? How could she stay knowing that she'd betrayed their trust?

She supposed she could argue that she hadn't known who Raul was when they'd been together. She could explain that she'd given him a false name to begin with and that it hadn't been until much later that she'd confessed who she really was. But what good would that do? she asked herself. It would still destroy whatever confidence Julia had in him, and, however she tried to avoid it, Ally couldn't forget that it had been she who had invited Raul into her room.

Of course, he could have refused. But he hadn't. And she didn't want to believe he'd only done it because he felt sorry for her. She had to wonder if he was in the habit of indulging in one-night stands. Did he often go away on his own? How well did Julia really know the man she intended to marry?

Ally blew out a breath. Raul's activities were really nothing to do with her. Not unless she intended to tell Suzanne and Peter about the night before, and somehow she knew she wouldn't do that. No matter how despicable his behaviour had been, she had to remain silent. She couldn't betray him without betraying herself.

Nevertheless, she couldn't stay here. Somehow, some way, she was going to have to find an excuse for leaving. It was devastating, but she was going to have to ring Sam and ask her to come up with a reason for her to return to England. She needn't tell her daughter the truth, of course. Just that things hadn't worked out as she'd planned and she was eager to come home.

She shuddered. The decision made, a feeling of intense depression swept over her. She'd so looked forward to coming here and now she was having to leave in the most cowardly way. It was bound to cause a rift with Suzanne, whatever excuse she came up with, and there was always the awful possibility that Raul might decide to confess to Julia and destroy what little credibility she had left.

She swallowed a little sickly. He wouldn't, she told herself. He wouldn't want to hurt the Davises any more than she did. What had happened had been an accident, an aberration, the result of propinquity, and an over-indulgence in alcohol on both their parts. It didn't matter that he'd known who she was when he'd made love to her. He'd obviously had a violent attack of conscience soon afterwards. That was why he'd left this morning before she was even awake.

Her lips twisted. Was that true? she wondered bitterly. Or was she only fooling herself? Where had his conscience been when he'd awakened her again and again all through the long hours of the night? He'd shown little concern for Julia when he'd been lying between her thighs, covering her face with hot passionate kisses. Oh, God! She trembled. No matter what happened, she knew she'd never forget him or his lovemaking.

But this was getting her nowhere. For tonight, at least, she was compelled to act as if she was looking forward to

her holiday. No one would believe that Sam would ring and
ask her to return home within hours of her arrival. Not unless
there was some dire emergency and that was something she
didn't want to convey. No, for the moment she had to behave normally, if that was at all possible. And hope that
Raul's family would be as eager to see him as Julia, thus
removing any danger of him turning up at Smuggler's Cove
tonight.

# CHAPTER FIVE

ALLY squeezed the salt water out of her hair and slung a towel about her shoulders. She'd enjoyed her swim. The water was cool and delicious at this time of day, but she'd decided it was getting too hot to stay on the beach any longer. It was only her second day of sunbathing and she didn't want to risk getting burned. Several of her fellow guests at the hotel were exhibiting the after-effects of over-exposure and the results looked very painful.

Fastening an ankle-length wrap that was patterned in vivid shades of green and purple about her waist, she picked up her sandals and started across the sand. One or two people from the hotel nodded to her as she passed and she reflected wistfully that in other circumstances she'd have considered herself very lucky to be here. Everyone was so nice, so friendly, and it was becoming incredibly easy to delude herself into thinking that perhaps she didn't have to leave, after all.

She hadn't seen Raul since her arrival, thank goodness. Perhaps he was ashamed of what had happened and was staying out of sight, she mused. Even the invitation to Finisterre had been postponed, saving Ally the need to find an excuse for declining that, too. Ostensibly, his mother was unwell, but Ally wondered if he'd told his family some half-truth about meeting her in London to explain why he didn't want to see her again.

But what could he have said? He could hardly have told his parents that he'd met her if he hadn't told Julia, and Suzanne's daughter would have told her mother in that case. In fact, Julia had been extremely friendly towards Ally, as if to make up for the offhand way she'd greeted her on her arrival, and Ally couldn't believe she knew anything about their encounter, whatever spin Raul might have put on it.

'Leaving so soon?'

She'd almost reached the flight of stone steps that wound up to the hotel when someone spoke to her, and, turning, she found another of the hotel guests behind her. She didn't know his name, but she had seen him in the lobby that morning, a man slightly older than herself, she guessed, with a lean athletic figure that was belied by his receding hairline.

'Yes,' Ally answered ruefully, indicating the slight redness that was evident on her bare shoulders. 'I'm afraid it's getting too hot for me.'

'And me,' agreed her companion. 'I'll never go brown, even if I stay out here all day. You're like me. Your skin's too fair for all this heat.'

Ally started to say that she hoped to go brown eventually and then changed her mind. She doubted if he was really interested. He was just being polite, making friends with a fellow holidaymaker. So instead, she said, 'Well, I'm not complaining. It's so beautiful here, and after the awful weather we've been having back home…'

'Oh, I know.' Her companion followed her up the steps, his arm brushing hers as she reached for the handrail. 'My name's Tom Adams, by the way. I just arrived yesterday afternoon.'

Ally nodded, managing not to react too violently to the deliberate way he kept close to her on the climb. 'Alison Sloan,' she said, not without some misgivings. And then, with rather more enthusiasm. 'Are you holidaying with your wife, Mr Adams?'

'I'm a widower.' They had reached the top of the stairs now and he fell into step beside her as they crossed the grass to the hotel. 'My wife died seven months ago,' he added. 'It was cancer, of course. Isn't it always? She was only forty-nine.'

'I'm so sorry.' Ally felt mean now for doubting his intentions. The man was obviously in need of sympathy and had had nothing more than that in mind. 'I suppose this is your first holiday without her. Were—were you married for long?'

'Twenty-eight years,' he replied, his hand cupping her elbow as they mounted the three shallow steps into the hotel. 'It's a long time, Mrs Sloan. Dare I ask if you're a widow yourself?'

Removing her elbow from his grasp, Ally tried not to feel too annoyed at the familiarity and shook her head. 'I'm divorced,' she said shortly. 'And now, if you'll excuse me, I'm going to take a shower. Salt water makes you feel so sticky, doesn't it?'

'I wouldn't know.' Tom Adams folded his arms with some diffidence. 'I'm not keen on swimming on my own.' Then, pushing his hands into the pockets of his shorts, he added, 'Perhaps we could meet up for a drink later? Not before lunch, of course. I'm sure you've got other things to do this morning. But, perhaps this evening?'

'Well, I—'

Ally was wondering what she could say to let him down without offending him when she became aware of someone watching them from the other side of the lobby. Several tall palms were gathered together in ornamental pots at the foot of the stairs that led up to the mezzanine area, and with a strange sense of *déjà vu* she saw a man standing in their shadow, his shoulder propped against the balustrade.

It was Raul.

For a moment, Ally lost the power of speech. Her throat dried and her tongue felt glued to the roof of her mouth. She must have lost colour, too, because the man beside her stepped towards her instinctively. Grasping her arm, he said, 'Are you all right, Mrs Sloan—Alison? Oh, dear, I think you have had too much sun, after all.'

'No. No, I'm fine. Really.'

Somehow Ally found her voice again, tugging her arm

urgently out of his possessive fingers. God, this was all she needed, she thought in anguish. For Raul to turn up and see her apparently getting too friendly with some other man. Not that she cared about his feelings, she told herself fiercely. She just hated the idea that he might feel some justification for the way he'd behaved.

'Are you sure?' Tom Adams didn't want to let her go and although he'd been forced to surrender his hold on her arm, when she moved away, he came after her. 'Let me see you up to your room.'

'That won't be necessary.' And then, as an afterthought, 'Um—thank you.' But Ally felt a hysterical sob rising in her throat at his words. History did repeat itself, after all.

'But you're shaking,' he insisted, and Ally closed her eyes against the uncharitable urge to push him away.

'I'm just tired,' she said, all too aware of their audience. 'I—if you'll excuse me.'

Tom Adams at last seemed to realise he wasn't doing his cause any good by persisting. 'Well, if you're certain,' he murmured, and she breathed more freely at the thought of making good her escape. Thankfully, the lifts were at this side of the lobby, enabling her to get up to her room without encountering Raul Ramirez. Now all she had to worry about was finding an acceptable excuse for Sam to give Suzanne as to why she had to return home. Immediately.

She'd pressed the button to summon the lift when Tom Adams came hurrying towards her again. 'About tonight,' he said, and Ally realised she was not going to shake him off. 'I understand that you might not want to talk about it now, but if you'll give me the number of your room, I'll give you a ring later on.'

'It's Mrs Sloan, isn't it?'

The voice was unmistakable. Rich and low, with just a hint of harshness to give it strength. Ally's skin feathered at its sensual assault on her nerves, but what troubled her most were the memories it so effortlessly evoked. Memories of

his hands on her skin, on her naked body, of his tongue
laving her swollen nipples and his powerful body penetrating
hers...

These pangs of sexual hunger were totally new to her.
Jeff had never made her feel the way she was feeling now.
But what scared her most was the power he had over her
shattered senses and the desperate ache she could feel deep
inside her that whatever happened she must hide from him.

'Oh—Raul,' she said, her eyes flickering towards him
quickly and away again. She refused to mimic his sarcastic
greeting and she was breaking every promise she'd made to
herself by even speaking to him again. But that fleeting appraisal had embraced everything about him, from the hair
that was visible above the opened collar of his sleeveless
body shirt to the muscled thighs below his denim shorts.
'Are you waiting for Julia?'

Tom Adams raised an enquiring brow as Raul's eyes
darkened with some emotion she couldn't identify. 'Do you
two know one another?' he asked, evidently deciding he had
the stronger claim to her attention, and Ally's lips pressed
together in sudden impatience.

'We're acquainted,' she responded shortly. She pressed
the button to summon the lift. Then, because something
more was expected of her, she added bitterly, 'Not very
well.'

Raul's mouth thinned. He turned to Tom Adams. 'Are you
and Mrs Sloan old friends?'

'No, we're not.' Before Tom Adams could reply, Ally
intervened. 'We met on the beach a few minutes ago,' she
told him, despising herself for the need she felt to make that
clear to him. But she had to defend her reputation, she
thought tightly, her expression hopefully mirroring the resentment she felt at his intrusion. The lift arrived and she
stepped gratefully into it. 'Excuse me.'

The doors were closing when Raul took her and Tom
Adams by surprise by joining her. His hand, ostensibly mov-

ing to press the button for the floor he wanted, blocked any attempt she might have made to open the doors again, and the last thing she saw was Tom Adams's shocked face before she was trapped in the enclosed cage of the lift with a man she both feared and despised.

'What the hell do you think you're doing?' she demanded, but Raul wasn't listening to her. With what she later decided was a suspicious familiarity with such things, he pressed the button that stalled the lift and then turned purposefully towards her.

Ally's heart skipped a beat at the look in his eyes, and she backed away from him. But not far. When her foot encountered the panelled wall behind her, she knew she had nowhere else to go. Raul came to put one hand at either side of her head, supporting himself and imprisoning her, and she gazed up at him with wide, apprehensive eyes.

'I—I'll scream,' she said, but evidently her threat didn't carry much conviction because he ignored it.

Bending towards her, he covered her lips with his and Ally's senses swam at the possessive pressure of his mouth. His tongue probed the seam of her lips, sought entrance, stroked the soft inner flesh with increasing urgency. His arms folded against the wall of the lift, bringing his lean frame against her, allowing her to feel what their kissing was doing to him. Then, his hands parted her wrap and his hairy thigh pushed intimately between her legs.

Weakness enveloped her. In the last couple of days she'd actually begun to hope that he might be too ashamed to show his face at the hotel and that if she could just avoid any invitations to his home she might be able to salvage something of her holiday. But she'd been wrong. Seeing him there in the lobby had exploded that belief. And now, with his hips against hers and his arousal pressing unmistakably into her stomach, she was made acutely aware that he had no shame. Unless she did something about it—like now—he was going to drag her down to his level.

Somehow, she managed to drag one hand up to her face. Turning her head, she pressed her knuckles against her lips. 'Please, don't do this.'

'Why not?' His mouth sought another target, nuzzling her palm before trailing erotic kisses across her cheek and down the side of her neck. 'You want me,' he said, his fingers finding the high-cut edge of her swimsuit and slipping intimately between her legs. He blew in her ear. 'You're wet.'

Ally caught her breath at this blatant provocation but she managed to answer him. 'I've—been swimming,' she got out unsteadily, but he didn't give up.

'Hot and wet,' he amended softly, stroking the pulsing nub of her womanhood. 'I do know the difference.'

Ally gave a strangled sob. 'Please,' she begged. 'Let me go. You're not being fair...'

'You have an old saying in your country,' he began, but she wouldn't let him finish.

'Let go of me,' she cried, her face contorted with emotion, and although she doubted her feelings had had anything to do with it, he abruptly released her and stepped back.

For a moment, Ally was too shocked to do anything. But then, when she came to her senses and reached for the button to start the lift again, once again he put himself between her and the panel. 'Wait.'

'Why should I?' Ally was shaking so badly she was amazed she was still standing. If she ever got out of here, she'd make sure she was never alone with him again, she thought grimly. 'I don't think we have anything more to say to one another.'

Raul rocked back against the wall of the lift behind him. 'You don't mean that,' he said flatly.

'I do mean it.' Ally was beyond thinking rationally. 'You—you disgust me. I disgust myself. If I had my way, I'd never set eyes on you again.'

Raul gave her a weary look. 'Really?'

'Yes, really.' Ally straightened, folding the wrap he had

dislodged more tightly about her waist. The fact that her actions didn't do anything to ease the throbbing between her legs was depressing but she'd get over it. 'I don't know how you have the nerve to stand there and pretend that it doesn't matter; that cheating on the woman you intend to marry means nothing to you. You're—you're despicable!'

'Did I say that it didn't matter?' he asked harshly. 'Did I say that I'm not ashamed of the way I've acted?'

Ally's jaw dropped. 'You don't mean to pretend you are?'

Raul's expression was bitter. 'What do you take me for?' he demanded. 'Do you think I do this sort of thing on a regular basis? As some kind of sick validation of my manhood, perhaps? Go on. Don't hold back. Tell it like it is.'

Ally swallowed. 'Then why did you—?'

'I don't know.' Raul spoke savagely. 'I don't know why I did it.' Then he backed up. 'Yes, I do.' He scowled. 'I did it because I couldn't help myself. There: that should give you some satisfaction. I made love to you because after I'd kissed you, after I'd touched you, I couldn't let you go.'

Ally moved her head disbelievingly from side to side. 'That's not true.'

Raul's mouth compressed. 'Why not?'

'Because I'm not like that,' said Ally fiercely. 'I'm no *femme fatale*. I'm not beautiful or glamorous. I'm just me! Late thirties and overweight, and my feet are too big. Men don't—well, until I spent that night with you, I'd never slept with anyone else but Jeff.'

'Which proves what, exactly?'

'Which proves—that apart from being too old for you, I'm not the kind of woman that—that any man would—' She broke off and then continued less emotively, 'I'm not like Suzanne or—or your mother, probably. I'm not sleek and sophisticated or—'

'You're talking rubbish,' said Raul impatiently and, although she tried to evade him, he grabbed her arm and forced her round to face her reflection in the narrow mirror behind her. 'Look at yourself,' he commanded. 'What do you see? Not the homely housewife you're describing, is it? Be honest with yourself, Ally. You're a lovely passionate woman. Age doesn't come into it. You're in your prime. Accept it. Enjoy it.'

Ally shook her head, but she couldn't avoid the image that confronted her. It was true, she thought. She didn't look much like the woman she was used to seeing in the bathroom mirror back home, but that was partly due to the sensual fullness of her mouth. Raul's kisses had left their mark; left her, too, with high colour in her usually pale cheeks. Even her damp hair had a tumbled sexuality about it. She looked—wanton, she decided unhappily, which was not something she would ever have believed about herself. Raul had done this, she realised, and she should hate him for it.

He had let her go to step back and slump against the wall opposite and now she turned to confront him with accusing eyes. 'And how am I supposed to enjoy it?' she demanded, combing her fingers through her hair in an effort to tame its tousled strands. 'By having an affair with you?'

'No!' With an exclamation of frustration, he pushed himself away from the wall. 'No,' he said again, angrily, his scowl causing deep furrows between his dark eyes. 'That's not what I meant at all. For God's sake, Ally, I don't like this situation any better than you do. It certainly wasn't my intention to get involved with someone else.'

Ally shrank away from his fury, her stomach cramping painfully at his harsh words. 'Then why did you?' she asked, hardly aware that by offering the question she was prolonging their isolation. 'Why did you?'

'Do you think I haven't asked myself that question?' he snapped. 'I should never have gone into your room; I know that now. The signs were there, goodness knows, but I chose to ignore them. I thought I was so cool, so in control of the situation. But I wasn't.'

Ally made a helpless gesture. 'I don't understand—'

'No, you don't,' he agreed flatly. He paused. 'Didn't you ever wonder why I should be staying at an airport hotel? I mean, I told you I'd been visiting the Boat Show. Surely you didn't think that that was my base for the whole time I was there?'

Ally shifted uneasily. 'I—didn't think about it.'

'No.' His expression was ironic. 'Well, I didn't. Stay at Heathrow, I mean. I stayed in London. I only spent that one night at the airport. As you did.'

'Then why—?'

'Do you want the truth?'

'Of course.' But Ally was apprehensive.

'Because Suzanne had spun this tale about her dear friend who was coming to visit. About what a rotten time you'd been having and how they were going to make sure you had a really good holiday.'

'I don't see—' Ally began, but he cut her off.

'I felt sorry for you,' he said brutally, and Ally's hand came to cover her mouth. 'I felt sorry for you,' he said again. 'I thought, Here's this pathetic little woman whose husband's deserted her, spending a lonely night at an unfamiliar hotel before facing a long, possibly nerve-racking flight the next day. Why don't I introduce myself to her, take her to dinner even, make her last night in England a pleasant one?'

Ally drew a trembling breath. 'Well, thank you for sharing that with me,' she said stiffly. 'I—I had wondered—'

'I said that was why I spent the night at the Regency,' Raul interrupted her harshly. 'I didn't say that that was what happened. It wasn't. For God's sake, Ally, you know that.'

'Do I?' Her voice was low.

'You should.' He thrust his balled fists into the pockets of his shorts. 'God, nothing worked out as I'd expected. I saw this attractive woman across the bar and I thought she might be you, but you said your name was Diana—'

Ally's cheeks burned. 'I did tell you my real name later.'

'I know you did. But by then it was too late.'

'Too late?' She was confused.

'Yeah.' He sighed. 'You see, I'd been attracted to—Diana, and I'd decided that I didn't care where Suzanne's friend was hiding herself.'

Ally stared at him. 'I don't believe you.'

'Nevertheless, it's the truth. Then, as you began talking about your family, I realised you might actually be the woman I had originally come to meet.' He paused. 'Surely you can see how the mix-up occurred?'

'I can see that it was too late for you to be truthful with me,' retorted Ally angrily. 'As soon as you knew who I was—'

'What would you have had me do?' He blew out a breath. 'You forget. By then I didn't want to tell you who I was.'

Ally quivered. 'Because you'd decided to take advantage of the situation?'

'You know better than that.' He scowled. 'Goddammit, Ally, I didn't force my way into your bedroom.'

'But you didn't refuse my invitation, did you?'

'No.' He conceded the point. 'But surely you must admit that what happened afterwards wasn't entirely my fault?'

'I don't want to talk about it.'

'Well, I do. Hell, why do you think I left you as I did? I knew that what I'd done was unforgivable, and I couldn't stand to face you in daylight.'

'So you sneaked away like a thief in the night!'

'If it pleases you to think of it like that.' Raul drew a deep breath. 'I'm not proud of what I did, Ally. That's why I want you to know—'

'I think we've said all there is to say,' Ally interrupted him tensely. She knew she couldn't take much more of this. Turning her head aside, she made her eyes search the control panel for the switch that would start the lift moving again. She had heard the hysterical note in her voice and, desper-

ately trying to tamp it down, she moved towards the doors.
'Is this the button?'

'Ally!'

'You don't have to worry,' she told him tensely. 'I'll be
leaving in a couple of days. I don't want to prolong this
fiasco any more than you do.' Her lips curled. 'Your dirty
little secret's safe with me.'

He swore then, but Ally wasn't listening. With a little
lurch, she'd set the lift on its upward journey and this time
he didn't attempt to intervene. When the doors opened at
the third floor he didn't move, and as there were two couples
waiting to get in, she was able to walk away without a back-
ward glance. She heard one of the men say something to
Raul about the unreliability of hotel lifts, but she didn't hear
his answer. With a shiver of apprehension, she opened the
door to her room and slipped inside with an aching sense of
relief...

# CHAPTER SIX

ALLY was sitting in the Patio Restaurant, making an effort to eat a chef's salad, when Suzanne slid into the chair opposite. Her friend was looking unusually hot and flustered and Ally hoped her appearance had nothing to do with her.

She'd already ascertained that Raul had left the premises. A casual chat with the receptionist had gleaned the information that Señor Ramirez had left an hour ago. Luisa, who was a very friendly girl, needed little encouragement to expound the merits of her employer's daughter's boyfriend. He was so nice and so good-looking, she'd exclaimed. Julia was so lucky to be going out with a man like him.

Not to mention the fact that his father was one of the richest men in the islands, Ally had appended cynically. Since being here, she'd discovered that both Suzanne and Peter regarded that as a major consideration. She'd been surprised at how mercenary they'd both become in middle age, and she could only assume it was the struggle they'd had to make the hotel a success that was colouring their judgement.

And after this morning...

But she didn't want to think about that. She'd already tried to ring her daughter, but apparently she was not yet home from work. Although she was still studying for a degree in Business Studies, Sam had taken a part-time job at a local fast food restaurant to supplement her student loan and, considering that England was five hours ahead of Nassau time, Ally had expected her to be in.

She'd catch her later, she assured herself, and, assuming an enquiring smile for Suzanne's benefit, she said, 'You look flushed.' She hesitated. 'Is something wrong?'

Suzanne shook her head. 'You don't want to hear about my troubles,' she said, raising a hand to summon the waiter and ordering herself a black coffee. She took a deep breath. 'I saw you going swimming earlier. Did you have a good time?'

Ally thought it was just as well Suzanne hadn't seen her coming back, but she nodded. 'It was wonderful,' she said warmly, realising that, whatever happened, she'd always be grateful to the Davises for inviting her here. 'The water's so warm.'

Suzanne turned to thank the waiter for the coffee he'd brought her, and then gave her friend a rueful look. 'It is delightful here, isn't it? We're so lucky to live in such beautiful surroundings.' She paused to tuck her hair behind her ears and sighed. 'I don't know what I'd do if I had to leave. The idea of going back to England...' She shuddered. 'I just can't imagine what we'd do.'

Ally frowned. 'Well, there's no question of that, is there?' She gestured about her. 'The hotel seems to be doing very well. It's obviously popular and—'

'Don't be deceived by appearances,' said Suzanne drily. 'Oh—we make a fair living; I'm not denying that. In the season, anyway. But it's not always as busy as this. When we first came here, it was a real struggle to survive.'

Ally stared at her. 'But that was years ago. Surely now you're in a position to sit back and enjoy it.'

'You'd think so, wouldn't you?' Suzanne's lips were tight. Then, with an impatient gesture, she dismissed the subject. 'Let's talk about something else.'

Ally bit her lip. 'Suzanne, if you and Peter are in some difficulty—'

'We're not.' She spoke brightly now. 'I'm just having one of my blue periods. They happen from time to time. Just ignore me.'

But Ally couldn't. Despite the fact that she was sure that this could have nothing to do with her, she had to pursue it.

'Suzanne, we're friends. We've been friends for thirty years. Surely you can tell me—'

'It's nothing, I tell you.' Suzanne's fingernails drummed a tattoo beside her cup. 'Tell me about your day. What are you going to do this afternoon?'

'Oh—' Ally was taken aback at having the tables turned on her. 'Well, I hadn't really thought about it.'

'Then you should.' Suzanne was her old confident self again. 'Have you been into San Cristobál yet?'

'No.' Ally shrugged. 'That is, only when you drove through it on our way here from the airport.'

'Pete will have to take you next time he goes to the market,' said Suzanne firmly. 'I'd offer to lend you the buggy, but it's a bit temperamental and I'd hate for you to have an accident while you're here.'

'I suppose I could hire a car,' murmured Ally, realising that it was unlikely she'd have the time to do either of those things. But Suzanne wasn't to know that, and it was good of her to offer her husband's services. 'I'll have to think about it.'

Suzanne was thoughtful. 'Yes, well, I suppose it would be better if you went one morning. Afternoons can be a little enervating. Have you got over your jet-lag yet?'

'Nearly.' Apart from waking up early in the mornings, Ally hadn't had any unpleasant after-effects of the journey. But then, she'd had more worrying things on her mind, she conceded tensely. Almost compulsively, she added, 'Um— where's Julia?'

Suzanne's expression changed. 'Don't ask.'

'Why?' Ally was anxious. 'She's all right, isn't she?'

Suzanne gave her a considering look. Then, she said tightly, 'Oh, yes. I suppose so. I'd really rather not talk about Julia either.'

Ally's stomach churned. 'I—I don't understand.'

'That's probably just as well.' Suzanne finished her coffee

and got abruptly to her feet. 'I've got to go, Ally. You know how it is: things to do, people to see.'

'Of course.'

But Ally wished she knew what had brought back that look of weary resignation to her friend's face. Oh, God, she thought, it couldn't have anything to do with Raul Ramirez, could it? But, no. She gave herself a mental shake. Suzanne was upset with Julia, not Raul. She mustn't become paranoid. Suzanne's problems were nothing to do with her. What had happened between herself and Raul had hurt no one but herself.

Ally had supper with the Davises that evening.

She had spent most of the afternoon trying to get in touch with her daughter, but without any success. She'd even considered trying to reach Ryan to see if he had any idea where his sister was. But her son lived with his girlfriend in Durham, where they were both attending university, and as Sam attended the university in Newcastle it was unlikely he'd know what she was doing. Besides, she reassured herself, she'd make contact with her daughter eventually; tomorrow, probably. If not, then surely Mark, Sam's boyfriend, would know where she was.

To her surprise, Julia had joined her parents on the lamplit private patio that adjoined the Davises' apartment. For the past couple of nights she'd been absent, spending the evening with Raul, Ally had assumed with a certain amount of suppressed emotion, but tonight she was perched on the low wall that edged the patio, nursing a cocktail and casting defiant glances in her parents' direction.

She perked up a little when she saw Ally, however, perhaps seeing her as a possible diversion. Patting the wall beside her, she said, 'Come and sit down, Aunt Ally. We haven't had a chance to have a proper chat since you arrived.'

Ally managed not to wince at the girl's greeting. It was

many years since Julia had used the honorary title but she was obviously trying to be friendly. 'All right,' she agreed, and after exchanging a doubtful look with Suzanne she seated herself on the wall. 'How are you this evening?'

'Better in health than temper, as Daddy always says,' replied Julia brightly. 'How about you? Are you enjoying your holiday?'

'Very much.' Ally accepted Peter's offer of a martini before continuing, 'It's just what you need in the middle of a cold English winter.'

'I bet.' Julia regarded her critically. 'You've obviously been sunbathing. It suits you.'

'Thank you.' Ally smiled. 'But I've got a long way to go before I can compete with you and your mother.'

'Mmm.' Julia gave Suzanne a guarded look. 'Well, if Mummy's brown, it's not through sunbathing. She never relaxes. She's always too busy, busy, busy!'

'It's just as well I am,' retorted her mother before Ally could respond. 'You wouldn't have had the opportunities you've had if it wasn't for the fact that your father and I have worked our fingers to the bone to support you.'

'Oh, Mum—'

'Suzanne!' It was her husband who intervened as he came to hand Ally her martini. A tall man, with thinning sandy hair and a comfortably expanding waistline, he was looking rather harassed this evening, and Ally guessed that whatever had been troubling her friend earlier had spilled over into the evening. 'I'm sure Ally's not interested in our family squabbles.' He forced a smile. 'Is that all right for you, my dear?'

Ally tasted her drink. 'Hmm, delicious, thanks,' she murmured, aware that Suzanne was regarding her husband with a faintly resentful air now. She hoped she was not going to be a party to a full-scale family row. 'It's a lovely evening.'

'Yes, isn't it?' Peter Davis propped one sandalled foot on the wall beside her, resting one arm across his knee as he looked out on the moonlit beach. 'We're very lucky living here.'

'As long as it lasts,' muttered his wife in an undertone, but everyone heard and Julia turned angry eyes on her mother.

'Can't you give it up?' she demanded. 'Just for one evening? As Daddy says, Aunt Ally doesn't want to hear what a disappointment to you I am. She came here to get away from all that, didn't you, Aunt Ally?'

'Oh, please…'

Ally didn't want to get involved and Peter straightened and turned to his daughter with reproving eyes. 'That's enough, Julia. I won't have you being insolent to your mother or trying to involve our guests.'

'But she—'

'Your mother only has your best interests at heart.'

'*Your* best interests, you mean,' retorted Julia, springing up from the wall and spilling a little of her cocktail over the short skirt of her taffeta dress in the process. 'Oh, look what you've made me do. It's ruined!'

'Well, don't expect to get another one as easily as you got that,' said her mother waspishly, and Ally stifled an inward groan. God, this was worse than she'd imagined and she was uneasily aware that, however much she might wish it wasn't so, Raul must be to blame.

'Why not?' Julia had turned on Suzanne now. 'I haven't said I won't marry Raul, have I? It's not my fault that Carlos finds me attractive.'

'It's your fault for encouraging him,' exclaimed her mother angrily. 'I trusted you, Julia. God knows what the two of you have been getting up to while Raul's been away.'

Julia gasped. 'We haven't been getting up to anything,' she snapped. 'We're friends, that's all. Friends! A concept you and Dad seem singularly incapable of grasping.'

'Now that really is enough.' Peter gave Ally an apologetic look. 'I'm sorry about this,' he said, 'but I will not have

Julia upsetting her mother all over again.' He turned to his daughter. 'If you can't keep a civil tongue in your head, I suggest you ask Maria to serve your supper in your room.'

Julia sniffed. To Ally's eyes, she looked perilously close to tears now. She was only a few years older than Sam and Ally wished she could tell the girl's parents to back off.

'I didn't upset Mummy,' she declared in a shaky voice. 'That was Raul. I didn't know he was going to be in such a filthy mood, did I? For heaven's sake, I've hardly seen him since he got back and then for him to be so mean, so sarcastic—'

'He was teasing you,' said Suzanne irritably. 'Haven't you known him long enough to know when to take him seriously or not?'

'Teasing me?' Julia was indignant. 'He was making fun of me, Mummy. He said I was spoilt. That I didn't have the first idea of what went on in the real world.'

'Well, you were rather unreasonable, weren't you?' her mother pointed out impatiently. 'Raul has responsibilities, Julia. He can't afford to spend all his time entertaining you.'

'I thought that was why he'd come to the hotel,' replied Julia defensively. 'If all he wanted to do was talk to Daddy, I don't see why he didn't just use the phone instead of driving all the way here.'

'I expect he had business in San Cristóbal,' said Suzanne at once. 'Since his mother's illness, his father has shifted more and more of the day-to-day running of the business onto his shoulders. You should remember that.'

'Well, I don't know what all the fuss is about,' muttered Julia crossly. 'Aren't I allowed to defend myself? For heaven's sake, all I said was—was—'

'That sometimes you wished you were dating Carlos and not him,' supplied her mother when she faltered. 'My God, I'm surprised he didn't tell you he'd had enough of you and your complaining.'

'You're exaggerating, Mummy.'

'So why aren't you dining with him this evening instead of spending a boring evening at home with your parents?' demanded Suzanne, and then pulled a horrified face. 'Oh, I'm sorry, Ally. I didn't mean that the way it came out. It's just—well—' she looked to her husband for support '—Julia knows we can't afford to offend the Ramirezes.'

'We haven't offended anyone, Mummy.' Julia gave an exasperated sigh. 'You're getting this out of all proportion. Good heavens, it isn't as if Raul's father owns the hotel. All right, so the Ramirezes are influential people, but most of our guests have never even heard of them.'

Ally saw the look Suzanne exchanged with her husband as Julia was speaking and wondered if there was more to her friend's concern than met the eye. At face value, Suzanne's reaction did seem a little extreme and Ally had the troubling notion that the girl's parents weren't being entirely honest with their daughter.

'Well, we'll see,' Suzanne murmured now, seeming to realise that her own dinner party was in danger of dying a painful death. 'Ally...' She turned to her friend. 'Let me refresh your drink.'

'No. Really.' Ally displayed her glass, which was still half full. 'I'm fine, thank you.' She took a deep breath. 'Something smells nice.'

'Oh, yes.' Suzanne glanced back at the private dining room behind her and then seemed to mentally square her shoulders before coming to sit in a cane chair nearby. 'Maria's a wonderful cook. I don't know what we—or the hotel—would do without her.'

Ally smiled. 'Let's hope you never have to find out,' she commented drily, and then realised too late that that was hardly the most tactful thing to say. 'I mean...'

'I know what you mean,' Suzanne assured her, leaning across to pat her arm. 'We've been friends for too many years for either of us to take offence at anything the other might say.' She gave Ally an appraising look, obviously trying to lighten the situation. 'You're looking very glamorous this evening. Have you arranged to meet Mr Adams in the bar later?'

'No, I haven't.' Ally could feel the colour creeping up her neck and sought refuge in her martini. She refused to admit that she'd taken any more trouble with her appearance this evening than she usually did. Her ankle-length black dress was excessively plain, she reminded herself, and she hadn't thought of Raul when she'd viewed her appearance in the mirror in her room upstairs. But she knew the dress complemented her height and shape, and she'd added a chiffon coat in shades of cream and bronze to accentuate the sun-bleached highlights in her hair. She licked her lips. 'How did you know I knew Tom Adams?'

'Oh, it's Tom, is it?' Suzanne was teasing. 'I must say you don't waste any time.' And then, noticing that her friend wasn't enjoying her banter, she gave a laugh. 'Relax, Ally. He asked me who you were this afternoon.'

Ally sighed anxiously, uneasily aware that she was holding her breath. She wondered what else Tom had said, and whether he'd mentioned the fact that he'd been out-manoeuvred by a much younger, darkly tanned individual, who'd spoken with a slight accent and who had got into the lift with her as well.

She was about to make some casual comment to distract her friend's attention, when she realised Suzanne's interest had waned. The other woman was watching her husband and her daughter as they moved closer together and Ally guessed she was wondering if Peter would succeed where she'd failed. Feeling a guilty surge of sympathy, Ally touched Suzanne's sleeve.

'It will be all right,' she said. 'You know what young people are like.' There was an awful irony in the words. 'Half the time they don't mean what they say.'

'What?' Suzanne turned to her with an absent expression. Then, comprehending that Ally had been sympathising with her, she shook her head. 'Oh, I know,' she murmured, as if impatient with herself. 'It's not the first time Julia and Raul have had words. I'm afraid she expects him to be always at her beck and call, but Raul's nobody's fool, is he?' Then, as if realising Ally had never met him, she added apologetically, 'Well, you'll find out for yourself soon enough. As soon as Isabel Ramirez is feeling better, we'll be expected to honour our invitation to Finisterre and you'll meet him and his brother.'

'Well, actually—' began Ally, wondering if this might be a good opportunity for her to intimate that she might not be staying as long as she'd intended. But before she could finish what she'd been about to say, Suzanne interrupted her.

'The trouble is,' she exclaimed, in a low impassioned voice, 'Julia doesn't really understand. She loves Raul, of course, but she thinks that the only reason we want her to marry him is because of who he is; because of the advantages it will give her as his wife.'

'And it's not?' Ally arched an enquiring brow.

'No.' Suzanne heaved a sigh. 'If only it were.' She paused, giving her friend a rueful look. 'Oh, I might as well tell you. Goodness knows, I need someone to confide in, someone I can trust.' She blew out a breath. 'We're in debt, Ally. We owe Raul's father a considerable amount of money, and if Julia doesn't marry Raul, I don't know what we're going to do.'

Ally stared at her. 'Suzanne! Surely you're exaggerating?'

'Now you sound like Julia,' said Suzanne drily. 'Believe me, I'm not. The situation—well, the situation is serious, and if we can't resolve it this way we may have to sell the hotel.'

Ally was appalled. 'But—why? What happened? I thought you said you were doing quite well.'

Suzanne pulled a wry face. 'I'm afraid we've never done as well as we claimed,' she admitted ruefully. 'When we first moved out here, we honestly wondered if we'd bitten off more than we could chew. I mean, we knew the hotel needed updating. That's why we got it so cheaply. But even then I don't think we'd taken all the extras into consideration.'

'Extras?'

'Oh, yes.' Suzanne grimaced. 'Even just ten years ago you could get away with *en suite* facilities and a simple menu, but times have changed. Nowadays holidaymakers expect so much more. We've had to install a swimming pool, buy jet skis, arrange for entertainment in the hotel. God, it never ends.'

'But surely you didn't do everything all at once?'

'Of course not.' Suzanne shook her head. 'The bank would never have stood for it. No, we just kept doing what we could, when we could, but it did mean that the loans we had just kept on getting bigger. And then we had the fire.'

Ally stared at her. 'A fire? In the hotel?'

'Just in the kitchen, thankfully.' Suzanne pulled a wry face. 'Unfortunately, we'd just spent a fortune on updating the cooking facilities and everything—everything was destroyed.'

'Oh, Suzanne!'

'But that wasn't the worst of it.' Suzanne hesitated. 'You see, we hadn't updated the insurance cover, and because they hadn't approved the alterations they refused to pay up.'

Ally didn't know what to say. 'I had no idea.'

'No.' Suzanne conceded the point. 'It's not something you tend to brag about. It was bad enough having to cancel bookings and close the hotel for five months. We really thought we might have to sell it and we were at our wits' end when Juan Ramirez offered to bail us out.'

Ally's tongue circled her lips. 'I see.'

Suzanne nodded. 'As I told you before, Julia and the boys had known one another for yonks, since they were just children, really, and although Peter and I have never been able to call Isabel and Juan friends, we have become much closer in recent years. Particularly since Raul and Julia have been together.'

'I see.'

'I doubt you do. Spanish families can be notoriously traditional, you know? I mean, we've dined at Finisterre more than half a dozen times in the last year, but I don't feel any closer to Isabel now than I did—what? Eighteen months ago.'

'Because of the loan, you mean?'

'No. Not because of the loan. I mean, until Raul started going away on business for his father, that hadn't been a problem. Juan had as good as hinted that once Julia and Raul were married he'd cancel the debt, and I'm afraid Pete and I have been speculating on the strength of it.'

'Oh, Suzanne!'

'Don't say it. I know. But until Raul began spending more and more time working for his father, Julia and he seemed perfectly happy together.'

'I suppose that's where—Carlos comes in?'

'That's right.' Suzanne made an impatient sound. 'He's been away for a couple of years, you see, completing his education in the United States, as Raul did. He's five years younger than his brother, and before he went away Julia had no time for him.'

'She's known them both for a long time, you say?' Ally ventured, and Suzanne inclined her head.

'Yes. I suppose it must be—oh, ten years since Julia was invited up to the house to play with Raul's sister, Sofía.'

'He has a sister, too?' Ally tried not to sound too interested.

'Yes,' replied Suzanne easily. 'They've been friends ever since.'

'Julia and Sofía?'

'All of them,' replied Suzanne ruefully. 'Carlos is only a year older than Julia and Raul must have been about eighteen at that time.'

Ally moistened her lips. 'So how old is Raul now?'

'Raul?' Suzanne frowned. 'Well, let's see: Julia is twenty-two so I suppose that makes Raul twenty-eight.' She gave it some consideration and then amended her assessment. 'No, he's twenty-nine. He had a birthday recently so he's a year older.' She grimaced. 'I wish I was twenty-nine. How much simpler life was then.'

Ally smiled, but it took an effort. Raul was almost exactly ten years younger than she was, she thought depressingly. He'd been just nine years old when she'd had the twins.

# CHAPTER SEVEN

SAM rang the following morning.

Ally was barely awake when the phone beside her bed began to peal and she groaned in protest as she fumbled for the receiver. 'Yes? Hello?'

'Mum? Mum, is that you?'

Sam's voice sounded almost painfully shrill and Ally winced. She wished now that Peter hadn't been so generous with the wine the night before. She knew she'd drunk more than she should but she'd been trying to put all thoughts of Raul Ramirez—and the things Suzanne had told her—out of her mind.

'Sam?' Ally struggled up against her pillows, her aching head a small price to pay for the relief of hearing her daughter's voice. 'Where have you been? I don't know how many times I rang the house yesterday.'

'I wondered if you'd been ringing.' Sam's tone was less penetrating now. 'Mrs Goddard said she'd heard the phone ringing when she passed the house.'

She would, thought Ally drily, recalling her elderly neighbour who spent much of her time ensconced in her sitting room window, watching the comings and goings in Penrose Terrace.

'Anyway, I'm sorry if you were worried,' Sam continued. 'But—well, something came up.'

'What?' Ally was wide-awake now, her own problems forgotten in her instinctive concern for her daughter. 'Is something wrong? You and Mark are getting on all right, aren't you?' She caught her breath as another thought occurred to her. 'Oh, God, it's not Ryan, is it?'

'Chill out, Mum. It's none of those things.' Sam was

laconic. 'When I said something came up, I didn't mean it was anything you should worry about.' She blew out a breath. 'So—are you having a good time? Is it a lovely place? I envy you, I really do. I'm hoping I can persuade Mark that we should lash out when we go on honeymoon. What do you think? Would Aunt Suzanne cut us a good deal?'

If they're still here, thought Ally uneasily. Then, 'Sam—'

'Anyway, why were you ringing me? Mrs Goddard said the phone had rung several times. That was why I thought of you. I couldn't think of anyone else who knows the number and doesn't know that I'm at college or working and you're away.'

Ally tried not to be impatient, but she was fairly sure that her daughter hadn't rung her for no reason. She felt a premonition of alarm. Something was wrong. She was sure of it. She could feel it in her bones. So why wasn't she feeling more optimistic about the fact that it looked as if she wasn't going to have to invent a reason to return to England?

'Sam,' she said now, trying to keep her voice even, 'never mind why I was trying to get in touch with you. You didn't ring me just to get a weather report on my holiday. As it happens—' she pulled a rueful face '—I'm having a very nice time. Or I was, until you rang.'

'Mum!'

'You know what I mean. Sam, please!' Ally sighed. 'I'm imagining all sorts of things. Put me out of my misery, do!'

There was silence for a moment and then Sam heaved a sigh. 'It's Dad,' she said, in a low voice, and Ally's jaw dropped. 'He's come back.'

'Come back?' Ally was momentarily dazed. 'What do you mean, he's come back? You mean—he and Kelly have come back to England?'

'No, I mean he's come back on his own,' replied Sam carefully. 'As in, he and Kelly have split up. At least, that's what he says. That's where I was all day yesterday. Talking to him at the hotel where he's staying.'

Ally was stunned. She couldn't believe what she was hearing. Jeff and Kelly had seemed rock-solid. But then, she reflected wryly, she and Jeff had seemed that way once, too.

'He says it's over,' went on Sam, as if realising her mother was too shocked to speak. 'Apparently they've been having problems ever since Dad moved to Toronto. According to him, the education system there is different from ours, and although he was a head of department here, he's just one of the minions there. And I think the fact that Kelly's position is higher than his has been something of a bone of contention between them. You know what Dad's like. He always needs to feel that he's top dog.'

Wasn't that the truth? Ally silently acknowledged that it was so. Jeff had always turned his thumbs down on the few occasions when she'd attempted to buck his authority. Like when the twins had started school and she'd suggested going back to college to get a degree. Jeff had insisted she had enough to do, looking after the house and caring for the family. That was why she'd only been able to get a job in an office now, having gained her secretarial skills at night school after the twins were old enough to be left alone.

'I can't believe it,' Ally said at last, pushing back the single sheet that was all that had covered her and swinging her legs over the side of the bed. It was hard to take it in. 'Did he say what he plans to do now?'

'Well—yes.' Sam was reluctant. 'He says he wants to put the past behind him and start again.' She took a breath. 'I'm so glad you're away, Mum. You've no idea how miffed he was when he found out. I think he expected you'd still be sitting here feeling sorry for yourself. When I told him where you were, he could hardly hide his indignation.'

'Sam!' Ally spoke in a strangled voice. 'He is your father. You're speaking about him as if he was a complete stranger.'

'He is to me,' retorted Sam at once. 'He didn't care about us when he took himself off to Canada, did he? He knew it was going to be hard for me and Ryan, just starting college and all, but he didn't give a damn about us.'

'Sam—'

'No. It's true, Mum, and you know it. All he cared about was Kelly and starting a new life with her. Well, it's not our fault if it hasn't worked out for him, and you can't blame me if I feel a certain amount of satisfaction now.'

'Oh, Sam—'

'Don't say "Oh, Sam" in that tone of voice, Mum.' Her daughter was impatient. 'Surely you feel the same?' She paused and, when her mother didn't say anything she added disbelievingly, 'My God, you're not feeling sorry for him, are you?'

'No—o.'

Ally drew out the word, trying to decide exactly how she did feel. Not glad, exactly, but, if she was completely honest, not sorry either. And if Jeff's plans hadn't worked out then he had only himself to blame.

'I should think not,' Sam was saying now, her young voice full of righteous indignation, and just for a moment Ally felt a pang of guilt. She wasn't wholly blameless herself, and if what had happened between her and Raul had been a totally one-off thing, happening after her divorce and not before it, had that been just her good fortune? Did she really know how she'd have reacted if she'd met Raul before she and Jeff had separated?

'So—he's going to look for another post in England?' she ventured after a moment and Sam made an angry sound.

'Not just in England,' she exclaimed resentfully. 'In Newcastle. Can you believe it? Like I said before, he thinks he can just take up where he left off. That's why I'm so glad you're out of the country. Hopefully, by the time you get back, he'll have got tired of hanging around here and taken himself off somewhere else. The further away, the better. I've told him he's unlikely to find a suitable position in this area, but he just says that until he's spoken to you he doesn't want to make any rash decisions.'

Ally stifled a groan. 'Why not?'

'Why do you think?' Sam sighed. 'He wants you back, Mum. He's realised what it's like having to do things for himself, and he doesn't like it. Let's face it: he's been spoiled. For years, you've waited on him hand and foot!'

'Hardly that.' Ally was defensive. She didn't like the thought that her daughter—and possibly her son as well—considered her a victim.

'Well, you did let him get away with murder,' Sam amended drily. 'But Kelly's not like that. She's far too full of herself to run after any man, least of all someone like Dad.'

Ally frowned. 'Why do you say that?'

'Oh, Mum.' Sam sighed again. 'It's not as if he'd win any beauty contests, would he? I mean, he's okay, I guess, but he is *forty* and Kelly's only twenty-eight.'

'You make forty sound ancient,' said Ally, feeling her age suddenly.

And already her stomach was churning at the prospect of having to face her ex-husband again. She had hoped never to have to see him again—and particularly not in circumstances like these, she thought unhappily. Sam was probably right. Jeff had dominated her for more years than she cared to remember and she was quite sure he'd expect an entirely different response from her from the one she was feeling now.

But it wasn't going to happen, she told herself fiercely. She didn't want him back. If the night she had spent with Raul had taught her nothing else, it had convinced her that the relationship she'd had with Jeff was not what she'd believed it to be. She'd loved him in her way, but she realised now that she'd loved the security he'd represented more.

When he'd destroyed that element of their marriage, he'd destroyed everything. She just hadn't accepted it before.

'I'm not saying forty's old, exactly,' Sam was continuing now, and Ally forced herself to concentrate on her daughter's words. 'But you have to admit, it's not young! That's all I meant.'

'Mmm.'

Ally tried to think. As she'd suspected, Sam had offered her the perfect excuse to curtail her holiday, and although Suzanne would no doubt object, she'd understand if Ally insisted on returning home.

'Anyway, I'm so glad you're having a good time,' Sam persisted. 'I bet Aunt Suzanne was really glad to see you. That's something you wouldn't have done if you'd still been married to Dad, remember that. He never encouraged you to have any friends. He was always afraid someone might displace him in your affections.'

'You're exaggerating, Sam.' Ally couldn't let her go on maligning her father. 'He wasn't that bad. He was just—a bit possessive, that's all.'

'A bit?' Sam snorted. But then, as if realising that her words were achieving the exact opposite to what she wanted, she backed off. 'All right,' she said. 'So, do you want me to give him a message? Like—get lost, or something a little more descriptive?'

'No.' Ally was appalled. 'Anything I have to say to your father, I'll say to him myself.'

'When?'

'When I get back, of course.'

Sam was wary. 'If he's still here, you mean.'

'Oh, he'll still be there.' Ally mentally squared her shoulders and took a deep breath. 'I think I'd better get the next available flight.'

'You can't!' Sam was horrified.

'Why can't I?'

'Because I told him you wouldn't be back until the end

of February. If you come back now, he's bound to think you're desperate to start again!'

It took an enormous effort of will for Ally to go down for breakfast.

Although she'd been forced to promise her daughter that she wouldn't make any hasty decisions without speaking to her again, her situation here was no less precarious because her ex-husband had decided to return home. She didn't really know why she was hesitating, why she was letting Sam's words influence her. She had been given the perfect excuse for cutting her holiday short, and even Suzanne couldn't be offended if she explained that she owed it to her children to find out what Jeff intended to do.

Her friend was bound to think she was a fool for doing anything to accommodate him, of course, but that couldn't be helped. At the end of the day, it was her decision, and right now she felt as if she was caught between a rock and a hard place.

All the same, Ally had to admit that she was reluctant to do anything to give Jeff the wrong impression. He had always been far too willing to take advantage of any weakness she exhibited, and hurrying back to England just because his affair with Kelly had apparently foundered was certainly not the most sensible thing to do. As Sam had said, he was sure to think she was eager to rekindle their relationship and, in those circumstances, it was going to be incredibly difficult to convince him otherwise.

Ally sighed as she crossed the lobby towards the Patio Restaurant. She wondered what Jeff would say if she told him the real reason why she'd wanted to leave San Cristobál. She doubted he'd believe her. So far as her ex-husband was concerned, she'd lost any claim to beauty years ago, and the idea that some other man—a younger man, no less—might have been irresistibly attracted to her would simply not strike him as feasible. He'd think she was making it up; that she was trying to pay him back for leaving her.

Of course, she thought ruefully, she couldn't tell him. Not without Sam finding out, too, and she couldn't bear it if her daughter decided she was no better than her father. Which left her in the unenviable position of not knowing where to turn.

'Mrs Sloan. Alison!'

The male voice was vaguely familiar and Ally turned to find Tom Adams approaching across the tiled marble floor. Her shoulders sagged. The last thing she needed was another problem in her life, she thought wearily. And the fact that Tom Adams had seen her and Raul together was an added complication.

'Hello,' she managed, pausing in the doorway to the open-air restaurant. 'It looks like another lovely morning.'

'Aren't they all?' Tom Adams smiled, but she could tell from his expression that he was remembering what had happened the day before. 'Are you breakfasting alone?'

'Why wouldn't I be?' Ally glanced out onto the sunlit patio. And then, because she felt obliged to try and put any possible thought of Raul out of his mind, she added, 'I suppose you've eaten.'

'Regrettably, I have.' But he seemed mollified by her subtle invitation. 'However, I'd be happy to—'

'Aunt Ally! Aunt Ally, wait!'

Julia's cry arrested them both and, glancing behind her, Ally was horrified to see Suzanne's daughter and the man she intended to marry coming towards them. In narrow black denims and a khaki shirt, open at the neck to expose the strong column of his throat, Raul looked disturbingly attractive and Ally glanced fearfully at Tom Adams, wondering what he was thinking. All she needed was for him to blurt out that she and Julia's boyfriend already knew one another and it would all be over.

But before Julia had a chance to say anything more, Tom

Adams made his excuses. 'I can see you're going to have company for breakfast after all,' he murmured in an undertone. 'But perhaps we can meet later. On the beach?'

'Oh—please.' Ally was so relieved that he wasn't going to cause trouble she could have hugged him, and her response was considerably warmer than it might have been because of it. 'The beach, yes,' she agreed, giving his arm a grateful squeeze. 'I'll look forward to it.'

Tom Adams gave a delighted smile and slipped away before the others reached her. But Ally was sure from the narrowing of Raul's dark eyes that he had noticed that affectionate exchange and despised her for it.

However, his expression revealed nothing but mild interest when Julia clutched Ally's hand and said, 'I wanted to catch you before we left.' She turned to the man beside her. 'This is Raul, Aunt Ally. You would have met him a couple of nights ago if we'd gone to Finisterre, but—well, he's here now, so that's all right. Raul, this is Mum's friend, Ally Sloan, from England. The one you were supposed to look out for at the airport. Perhaps she wouldn't mind if you called her Aunt Ally, too.'

Ally cringed at Julia's patronising words but to her relief Raul rescued her from complete ignominy. 'I don't think Mrs Sloan looks old enough to be your aunt, let alone mine,' he remarked drily, holding out his hand, and Ally was forced to take it. Then, with terrifying candour, he said, 'Besides, I believe we have met before, Mrs Sloan.' And, as the colour drained out of Ally's face, he added, 'If I'm not mistaken, we shared the lift yesterday afternoon.'

Julia stared at him. 'You never said,' she pouted, as Ally struggled to retain her composure, and Raul shrugged.

'I didn't know who Mrs Sloan was, did I?' he replied reasonably. 'It was when I went up to the office to speak to your father.' He turned back to Ally. 'Small world.'

'Yes. Isn't it?' Ally could feel the blood pouring back into her cheeks again, and she pulled her hand out of his grasp with careful determination. 'How—nice to see you again.'

The words almost choked her and she was sure he knew it. But thankfully Julia seemed to notice nothing amiss. 'Oh, well,' she said, slipping her hand into his. 'I suppose we'd better get going. Raul's taking me sailing this morning, Aunt Ally. That's what he does for a living, don't you, darling? He runs his father's charter company. They charter yachts to companies and to people who want the thrill of sailing, but can't afford to buy their own.'

'Which must be the best part of the world,' remarked Ally shortly, trying not to resent his smug complacence. Then, forcing a smile, she added, 'Well, have a good day. I'll think about you when I'm tucking into some of Maria's blueberry pancakes.'

Of course, she wouldn't. Well, she might think of them, she acknowledged, but seeing them together had robbed her of what little appetite she'd had, and she wondered if it wouldn't be simpler just to tell Suzanne she was leaving and get it over with. At least the decision would be made, for good or evil.

'Perhaps Mrs Sloan might like to join us.'

Raul's careless invitation caught her completely unprepared and she was relieved and hardly surprised when Julia took exception to it.

'You're not serious!' she exclaimed, apparently not at all averse to offending the older woman. 'Aunt Ally doesn't know anything about boats! I doubt if she's been on anything larger than a motor boat in her entire life.'

'All the more reason for her to learn,' observed Raul mildly and Ally could see that Julia was seething with repressed emotion.

'Why are you doing this—?' she began angrily, but before their exchange could get out of hand, Ally intervened.

'Julia's right,' she said, even though the girl's words had been unnecessarily hurtful. Which was ridiculous, she acknowledged impatiently, her eyes darting away from Raul's dark challenging gaze. For God's sake, it wasn't as if she wanted to spend the day with them. 'I'm—no sailor,' she continued doggedly. 'Besides—' she made a gesture in the direction Tom had taken '—I've promised to join Mr Adams after breakfast.' Her lips tightened. 'But thank you for the invitation.'

'Some other time, perhaps,' murmured Raul, ignoring Julia's agitation. 'I understand you're staying for several weeks.'

'Well—I'm not sure how long—'

Ally didn't want to get into that with him, but he immediately understood her ambivalence. And called her on it.

'No?' he queried, as if any doubts she was having were news to him. 'Surely you're not thinking of cutting your holiday short?'

Ally swallowed, forced to look at him or risk arousing Julia's curiosity—or worse. 'I—it may be necessary for me to return to England sooner than I anticipated,' she murmured awkwardly, and he smiled.

'I hope not.' His determination was almost frightening. 'And Julia has forgotten to tell you that I came to bring an invitation from my parents for you all to dine at Finisterre in two days' time. As Julia said, an earlier invitation had to be cancelled and my mother is so looking forward to meeting you.'

'Well—'

'He's only teasing you, Aunt Ally.' Although Julia spoke tersely she had evidently come to the conclusion that Raul must be teasing her, too. 'In any case, you can't leave yet. After waiting for goodness knows how many years for you to come and visit us, Mum would never forgive you if you decided you'd rather go back to an English winter than stay here.'

Ally felt trapped. She had no idea what Raul's game was but she was fairly sure he had not been teasing. Which meant—what? That he was enjoying tormenting her? That she couldn't trust him not to say anything if she opposed his will?

That he wanted her to stay?

# CHAPTER EIGHT

ALLY slept badly that night and awakened the next morning stiff and unrested. The muscles in her shoulders felt tight and knotted, and there was the uneasy flutter of apprehension in her stomach. Stepping into the shower cubicle, she ran the water as hot as she dared in an effort to loosen the tension in her neck and then switched to a cooler temperature before stepping out.

What was she going to do?

As she wrapped herself in one of the soft towelling bath sheets, she made another attempt to consider her options and decided they were narrowing by the day. She had thought it was up to her whether she risked offending Suzanne by returning home, but it wasn't. Raul had made it his business, too. And, on top of that, there was her daughter begging her not to ruin her holiday, who wouldn't understand why her mother appeared to be stalling over making a decision about a man who hadn't considered her feelings in the past.

Tom Adams would be pleased, she reflected ruefully. He had been waiting for her the day before when she'd eventually made her way down to the beach. He must have wondered what had taken her so long, but, after that scene with Raul and Julia, she hadn't felt much like socialising with anyone. She'd made some excuse about having to wait to be served in the restaurant, when in actual fact all she'd done was order coffee and that had been delivered almost immediately.

Nevertheless, she couldn't deny that she had felt a certain amount of security in Tom's company, a belief that while she was with him Raul would keep his distance. An unnecessary conviction in the circumstances, she acknowledged drily. Raul and Julia had gone sailing. The chances of seeing him again that day had been slim and she'd known it.

And, she remembered, Tom had offered no protection that morning when Raul had cornered her by the lifts. Raul hadn't shown much concern for the other man then, and she could only assume that seeing her so unexpectedly had caused him to act totally out of character. Which was probably why he'd covered himself by saying they'd met before when Julia had introduced them. Raul was nothing if not thorough in everything he did.

All the same, Ally hoped she wasn't going to have to spend the whole of the holiday keeping Tom Adams company. He was a nice man; there was no doubting that. But he was too much like Jeff for her liking and she had no desire for him to get the wrong impression.

The phone rang as she was leaving her room to go down for breakfast.

Sam, she thought at once, coming back into the room again. She guessed her daughter had chosen this time to be sure of catching her in, as she'd done the previous day.

Or it could be Tom Adams. As she reached for the phone, she recalled that he'd coaxed her room number out of her the afternoon before. Thank goodness she'd been able to say that she was having supper with Suzanne and Peter again, she thought ruefully. Otherwise, he'd have monopolised her whole day.

Still, right now she couldn't take the chance of not answering in case it was Sam. She'd been going to ring her daughter anyway, to tell her that she'd decided not to rush back after all. She wasn't promising to spend the next three weeks in San Cristobál, as she'd originally intended, of course, but Sam needn't know that. One day at a time, she told herself, lifting the receiver.

'Hello?'

'Good morning, Ally.'

It was Raul. She'd have known his voice anywhere, she

thought, wishing she had the courage to slam the phone
down again.

'What do you want?'

She was less than gracious and she heard the amusement
in his tone as he said, 'To speak to you. What else? Did you
have a good day yesterday? I saw you on the beach with
your elderly admirer. Tell me, has he appointed himself your
protector against undesirable characters like myself?'

Ally stiffened. 'You said it.'

'You wound me.'

'No, I don't.' She despised herself for the frisson of excitement his words had given her. 'And Tom's not elderly.
He's nearer my age than you are.'

'I don't think so.' Raul's voice lost some of its humorous
appeal. 'He's at least twenty years older than you are. There
are only a handful of years between us.' He paused. 'If you
feel it's necessary to count.'

'There are ten years between us,' said Ally fiercely. And
then, knowing she would hate herself for it, she asked, 'How
did you see me on the beach anyway? I thought you and
Julia were going sailing.'

'We did.' His tone lightened again. 'The conditions
weren't suitable. We had to come back. But I'm flattered
that you were interested enough to find out how old I am.
That pleases me. It pleases me a lot.'

Ally felt a shiver of anticipation slide down her spine. 'It
shouldn't.' She drew a breath. 'And what do you mean, the
conditions weren't suitable for sailing? There was a fairly
stiff breeze blowing off the water.'

'Are you suggesting that there was another reason why
we came back?'

'I don't know, do I?'

His attractive voice deepened. 'Perhaps you're thinking I
came back to see you.'

'No.' Ally's tongue circled her dry lips. 'I wouldn't think
a thing like that.'

'Perhaps not.' He paused. 'In any event, I didn't ring to discuss what happened yesterday. I want to know what you have planned for this morning.'

'This morning?' Ally wished she had a ready answer. 'I— I'm not sure—'

'Obviously you have nothing planned,' he remarked drily. 'I'll pick you up in—shall we say, an hour?'

'You can't.'

'Why can't I?'

'I don't want to go anywhere with you.'

'Don't you?'

'No.' Ally swallowed. 'In any case, Julia—'

'Julia is spending time in the beauty parlour this morning,' he informed her flatly. 'She told me so last evening. She is anxious to look her best for my mother's supper party tomorrow evening.'

'Then perhaps I should try and make an appointment, too,' said Ally at once. 'As you insist on me attending the party.' She caught her breath. 'Why did you do that? You must have known how I would feel.'

'I thought I did,' he responded softly. Then, almost detachedly, 'I don't want you to go back to England. I want you to stay here.'

Ally was trembling. 'Why? *Why?*'

'I'll tell you later. Bring a hat. The sun can be merciless on the water.'

'But I can't,' she wailed, but he wasn't listening to her.

'Be at the gate at nine o'clock,' he told her steadily. 'Don't let me down.'

He rang off before she could tell him she wouldn't be there. She was left holding the receiver, the dial tone buzzing emptily in her ear. Slamming it back onto its rest, she stared at it for several seconds, half hoping he would ring back and give her the chance to tell him she wasn't coming. But he didn't. The phone remained ominously silent and as she hadn't the first idea where he'd rung from, she was helpless.

Her cheeks were burning and almost involuntarily she
moved towards the vanity mirror and stared at her reflection.
This couldn't be happening to her, she thought, even while
her mind was registering the pros and cons of what she was
wearing and whether she ought to change into something
else. Whatever the outcome, she didn't have a wardrobe full
of designer gear to choose from. But her cream polo shirt
and matching cotton shorts had definitely seen better days.
She was always self-conscious about her generous hips, too.
But her legs were decent. Perhaps they'd distract his eyes
from—

Wait!

She brought herself up sharply. What was she thinking?
She wasn't even going to meet him. *Right?* Right. All this
was purely hypothetical because she was going to stay right
here in her room until lunchtime. Until there was no chance
of meeting him at all.

She ran a hand round the back of her neck and found it
damp. Oh, great! She was sweating again. He only had to
get on the phone and her body reacted like it did when she'd
been too long in the sun. He reduced her to a quivering mass
of nerves and senses, incapable of handling him, incapable
of controlling herself.

It had to stop.

Stripping off her clothes again, she marched back into the
shower and turned on the cold tap, not coming out again
until she was chilled to the bone. Then, tossing the polo shirt
and shorts into the laundry bag, she dressed in a plain, short-
sleeved cotton shirt and a denim skirt whose hem hovered
a couple of inches above her knee. Smart, without being too
formal, she decided, with some satisfaction. And deliciously
cool in the draught of air coming from the air-conditioning
system.

The phone rang again.

Ally sank down weakly onto the side of the bed, staring
at the phone with almost morbid fascination. And then, be-

cause once again it could be Sam, she reached for the receiver.

'Is that you, Alison?'

Who else?

Ally wanted to groan aloud. 'Hello, Tom,' she managed tightly. 'Look, I'm afraid I can't talk now. I was just about to go into the shower.' *Liar!* 'So can I—?'

'That's all right. I won't keep you.' He was depressingly understanding. 'I'm not dressed myself yet, actually. I slept in.'

'Oh, well—'

'Anyway, I wondered if we might do something today. Together. I haven't seen much of the island yet, and I know you haven't, and I thought if I hired a car—'

'I can't.' Ally knew she might regret it, but there was no way she could spend another day in Tom Adams's company. He meant well, but his fussy ways would drive her up the wall. Ignoring the voice of conscience, she added recklessly, 'I've—er—I've already made arrangements to go out with someone else.'

'You have?' He was clearly taken aback and she sensed the wave of injured pride that accompanied his words. 'Anyone I know?'

Ally gasped. He was even more like Jeff than she'd imagined. 'I—no,' she said firmly. 'And now I must go.'

'Of course.' But he didn't attempt to hide his disappointment at her answer. 'Well, have a nice day.'

She was sure he hoped she wouldn't, but that didn't solve her problem. She was now in the position of wanting to avoid two men and she realised that once again she'd backed herself into a corner.

So, she could either stay here and have Suzanne thinking she was unwell, or she could do the unthinkable and meet Raul.

She blew out a breath. What a choice! How could she spend the morning with Raul when he was the man Julia was going to marry? She'd already done more than enough to cause a rift between them, and the fact that she'd been innocent of any wrongdoing was not a satisfactory defence.

She sighed, moving towards the windows that were open onto the balcony, gazing wistfully at the view. It was so beautiful out there. Was she really going to waste a whole day of her holiday locked up here just because she was too timid to stand up for herself?

No!

Turning back into the bedroom, she picked up her bag and sunglasses and started for the door. She was going to get some breakfast, and if Tom Adams—or Raul, for that matter—didn't like it, it was just too bad.

Nevertheless, she looked about her a little nervously when she emerged from the lift in the lobby. It was easy to be brave before the event, but she felt less confident now.

'Hey, Ally!'

Suzanne's call was momentarily mind-numbing, but she managed to turn and face her friend without looking too distressed. 'Good morning.'

'Good morning.' Suzanne gazed at her with some satisfaction. 'You look nice. I think you're actually getting a bit of a tan.'

'I think so, too,' said Ally, wondering why her friend appeared a little anxious. She took a nervous breath. 'Is something wrong?'

'Not wrong, no.' Suzanne shook her head. 'As a matter of fact, I was just on my way up to your room. I had a favour to ask.'

'A favour.' A ripple of apprehension feathered across Ally's skin. 'Of course. What is it?'

'You'd better hear what it is before you commit yourself,' declared Suzanne, tucking her hand into her friend's arm. 'How do you fancy spending the morning with Raul?'

'With *Raul*?'

A little of her consternation must have shown in her face

because Suzanne said quickly, 'I know. It's a lot to ask, but he seems to think you might enjoy it. Julia would have gone along, too, of course, but she's having her hair done, and Pete and I are simply up to our eyes—'

Ally wet her parched lips. 'Raul asked you to ask me?' she probed weakly, and Suzanne gave a rueful nod.

'Well, he would, wouldn't he? I mean, he hardly knows you. Julia said you'd spoken to him briefly the day after you arrived, and I know the three of you had a few words yesterday morning before he and Julia went out, but you know what his family is like. Everything has to be done so—so formally.'

Ally didn't know what to say. Well, she did, but she couldn't say it, she thought grimly, realising that she had underestimated him.

'I mean, he's very nice,' went on Suzanne, apparently deciding that Ally needed some encouragement. 'And I'm sure you'll enjoy seeing more of the island. You'd be doing me a favour, as I say. I shouldn't like to offend him.'

'No.' Ally's tone was flat. After what Suzanne had told her two nights ago, she was hardly surprised. 'I can understand that.'

'I knew you would.' Suzanne squeezed her arm. 'Besides, look at it positively: some women would be flattered that a man as young and personable as Raul should take the trouble to entertain you. I mean, as far as he's concerned, you're just his girlfriend's aunt.'

I'm not his girlfriend's aunt, thought Ally desperately. And you don't know the half of it! If you did, this is the last thing you'd suggest.

'Well, what do you say?'

Suzanne was looking at her expectantly, and Ally didn't see how she could refuse. Or that was her excuse, she realised despairingly. If she was really honest wouldn't she simply admit that Suzanne had solved the problem? That she really wanted to go?

'I—' She glanced at her watch. It was already half-past eight. 'I haven't had breakfast yet.'

'No problem.' Suzanne put an arm about her waist and urged her across the lobby and into the Patio Restaurant. 'I'll have Martin serve you right away. What would you like? Eggs and bacon? Pancakes?'

'Just toast,' said Ally weakly, realising she had tacitly accepted Raul's invitation. And, by so doing, once again he was getting his way. Dear God, was it only a week ago that the most troublesome problem on her schedule had been deciding what she was going to wear to travel in? Since then, her life had resembled a roller-coaster ride.

# CHAPTER NINE

ALLY was struggling to swallow the last mouthful of toast and lime jelly when she saw Raul crossing the restaurant towards her. In a dark blue collarless body-fitting shirt and matching shorts, he looked relaxed and amazingly familiar, and Ally felt her taste glands dry up.

A surreptitious glance at her watch told her that it was barely nine o'clock, and she quickly swallowed the rest of her coffee to ease the remains of the toast down her throat.

'Hi,' he said, pulling out a chair from the table and swinging it round so that he could straddle it. 'Are you ready?'

Aware that Raul's arrival had attracted an embarrassing amount of attention, Ally looked impatiently about her. 'As I'll ever be, I suppose,' she said ungraciously. 'Tell me, do you often employ the services of a third party to arrange your dates for you?'

Raul's lips twitched. 'Is that what this is? A date?'

Ally coloured. She couldn't help it. 'What else?' she asked shortly, wishing she had more experience with his sex. 'Shall we go?'

'Why not?' He got up from his seat. 'I like a woman who knows what she wants and goes after it.'

Ally gave him a glare. 'Don't,' she said tensely. 'Just don't.' And then, aware that she was never going to get the better of him, she pushed back her chair and stalked angrily out of the restaurant.

The cream convertible Carlos had been driving that day at the airport was waiting at the front of the hotel. Evidently Raul had decided there was no need to leave his car at the gates when Ally had Suzanne's endorsement for her trip, and she halted at the top of the steps, looking down at it with some trepidation.

'Is this yours?'

'It belongs to Carlos,' he told her, going lightly down the steps to open the passenger door. 'Do you like it?'

'It's—flashy,' she said, using the least complimentary adjective she could think of. Following him, she got into the front seat, taking care not to expose any more thigh than was absolutely necessary.

Raul's lips twitched again. 'You should have worn shorts,' he commented, walking round the car and getting in beside her. His bare arm brushed hers and she jerked away. 'Never mind. I'm sure we can find you something more suitable to wear.'

'I don't need anything more suitable,' retorted Ally, remembering the shirt and shorts she'd had to cast into the laundry bag. 'Where are we going?'

Raul started the car's engine and swung away down the short drive. 'You know where we're going,' he said, his hands very brown and competent on the wheel. 'Oh—and I told you to bring a hat.'

'It may interest you to know that I had no intention of meeting you this morning,' declared Ally crossly, wishing her heart wasn't beating quite so fast and that the palms of her hands didn't feel quite so slick on the strap of her bag. 'And I don't wear a hat.'

Raul shrugged. 'You should.' He paused. 'And I knew you might not come. That was why I asked Suzanne to speak to you.'

'To blackmail me?' Ally knew she was overreacting, but she couldn't seem to stop herself. 'You have no shame.'

Raul drew a deep breath. 'I didn't know you felt so strongly about it.' He halted as they reached the road that ran past the hotel and turned to look at her. 'Do you want to go back?'

Ally was taken aback. 'We—I can't.'

'Yes, you can. I'll take you back.' His lips twisted. 'Never let it be said that I had to blackmail you to come out with me.'

Ally closed her eyes. 'I never said that.'

'Yes, you did.'

'Well, I didn't mean it. Not literally.' She opened her eyes again. 'Besides, Suzanne would be sure to think I'd offended you.'

'You have.' His tone was flat. 'But I'd make some excuse if that's what you want.'

Ally groaned. 'Oh, you know what I mean, what I'm trying to say. I don't want to—to offend you, but we—we shouldn't be doing this.'

Raul's eyes darkened. 'Does that mean that you don't want to go back?'

'No. *Yes.*' Ally gazed at him, her expression open and vulnerable. 'Oh, I suppose you think I'm stupid.'

'No. Just—incredibly sexy,' he replied softly, dragging his eyes from hers with an obvious effort. 'And far too innocent for your own good.'

Sexy! Ally swallowed incredulously, and, taking her silence as acquiescence, Raul swung out onto the coast road. She shook her head. There was no turning back now. However reckless she was being, she was committed to spending the morning with him.

If she hadn't been so self-conscious, Ally would have enjoyed the ride to the marina where Raul told her many of his father's craft were moored. It was the first time she'd left the hotel since her arrival and once again she was enchanted by the island's beauty. Unfortunately, however, her anxieties about what she was doing overshadowed her enjoyment. No change there, then, she thought wryly.

Despite the fact that Suzanne had sanctioned this outing, she couldn't relax. Even though it had succeeded in driving any worries about her ex-husband to the back of her mind. And now she had time to think again, she wished that she'd rung her daughter before leaving. Even though Sam had urged her not to return home immediately, she would expect her mother to keep her in touch with her plans and not behave as if she was a totally free agent.

'What are you thinking about?'

Raul's question brought the realisation that she had been torturing the strap of her handbag, and, releasing it, she pressed her hands together between her bare knees.

'This and that,' she answered, after a moment, and Raul gave her a retiring look.

'Yeah, right.' His jaw compressed. 'Are you sure you don't want to go back?'

'No.' Ally cast him an indignant look. 'I do think about other things besides you, you know.'

Raul gave a small smile. 'I'm pleased to hear it.'

'Now you're teasing me again,' she said crossly. 'As a matter of fact I was thinking about—Jeff.'

'Your ex-husband?' He hadn't forgotten anything. 'Why am I not flattered?'

'Don't be sarcastic.' Ally sighed. 'I wasn't thinking about him in that way.'

'What way?'

Too late she realised how provocative her words had sounded. '*Any* way,' she amended shortly. Then, aware that although his eyes were on the road she had his full attention, she added, 'He's come back.'

'Come back?'

The road was narrowing ahead of them, winding down to sea level where a small marina provided a mooring for several vessels, large and small alike. Ally could hear the gentle chiming of mooring buoys, the susurration of the tide as it lapped against the wooden docks, could see the brilliance of the sun on the water. Tall masts rose and fell in stately elegance, their sails reefed and stowed away. There were a few people about but a lot of the slips were empty and Ally guessed that many of the chartered craft were away for several days or weeks at a time.

'Come back?' Raul repeated, after he'd negotiated the twists and turns of the road and was reversing the big car into a convenient parking bay. He brought the vehicle to a halt and turned to look at her. 'How do you know?'

'Sam rang me. My daughter, remember?'

'I remember who Sam is,' he agreed shortly, and she tried not to be impressed by his recall. 'When did she ring you?'

'Yesterday morning,' said Ally unwillingly. 'Not that it's any business of yours. You asked what I was thinking and I told you.'

'So you did.' Raul's lips twisted. 'Dare I ask if you knew he was returning.'

'Of course I didn't know,' exclaimed Ally, winding the strap of her bag around her hand again. 'How could I? As far as I was aware, he and Kelly were rock-solid.'

'As you and he once were,' remarked Raul drily, and Ally caught her breath.

'No. Not like Jeff and me.' She hesitated. 'I was only eighteen when I married Jeff.'

Raul regarded her quizzically. 'But you must have believed your relationship was sound,' he said. 'Or—'

'I was pregnant,' said Ally stiffly, her eyes bright with hot embarrassment. 'You might want to revise that opinion you have of me.'

Raul gave her an impatient look and pulled the keys out of the ignition. 'Let's go,' he said, and she couldn't be sure that his sudden abruptness was the result of his words or hers. Whatever, after getting out of the car and opening the door, he went round to the back of the car and removed what appeared to be a picnic basket from the boot. 'Follow me.'

They crossed the sunlit quay, Ally having to quicken her step to keep up with him. They walked out along a slatted planked dock where every knot in the woodwork was a po-

tential hazard to her sandal-clad feet. She should have worn
her trainers, she mused ruefully. But then, she hadn't known
that she was going to be expected to follow Raul along a
narrow boardwalk with the uneasy suspicion that she had
annoyed him again.

She'd stopped to adjust the strap at her heel when he
disappeared. One minute he was about a dozen yards ahead
of her and the next he was gone. She stumbled on, wondering if he'd done it deliberately. Probably, she decided
tensely. Perhaps he was hoping she'd just give up and go
back to the hotel.

'Ally!'

His voice startled her, and she teetered round on her high
heels not sure where the call had come from. Then she saw
him. He was standing on the deck of a gleaming vessel
whose tall masts and streamlined hull looked far too big for
one person to handle.

But swinging round had been a mistake. Instead of supporting her, one of her heels slipped between the slats, and,
before she could save herself, she lost her balance.

The word Raul used then was not a complimentary one,
she knew that. But, with the agility of a man in superb phys-
ical condition, he vaulted onto the dock and sprinted the few
feet between the slip and where she was struggling to save
herself from falling into the water.

'Crazy woman,' he muttered, when he had her safely in
his arms, and, swinging her up against his chest, he carried
her back to the yacht and across the short gangway onto the
deck.

Ally was too shocked to offer any protest. The image of
what might have happened if she'd fallen was all too vivid
in her mind. The spars of wood that jutted up along the jetty
were an obvious danger, but she was aware of how easy it
would have been to fall between the yacht and its mooring.
To imagine herself crushed by the movement of the heavy

vessel made her feel sick and, when Raul lowered her to her feet, she was still trembling.

'God,' he said, his hands moving up to cradle her face and turn it up to his. But although his touch revealed how shaken he himself was by what had so nearly happened, his words were harsh and unsympathetic. 'What the hell are you wearing high heels for?'

Ally tried to summon up some indignation. 'I didn't know I was going to have to walk a tightrope, did I?' she exclaimed, wobbling again as she felt the deck move beneath her feet. 'It wasn't my fault.'

'It's not a tightrope,' muttered Raul irritably, his fingers probing the hollows behind her ears. 'Dammit, it's just a dock, a wooden pier that anyone with half a brain would be able to negotiate.'

'Then obviously I don't even have half a brain,' said Ally tremulously, lifting her hands to push him away. But, before she could stop it, his mouth found hers.

'Crazy woman,' he said again, against her lips, and then his tongue was pushing past her teeth, seeking the undefended vulnerability of her mouth.

Ally's senses swam. She couldn't help it. Already beating fast from the narrow escape she'd had moments before, her heart went into overdrive, thundering in her ears and sending the blood surging to the surface of her skin.

She knew she ought to stop him, to beat her fists against him and defend herself against his totally unfair assault, but she didn't. She couldn't. In a rare moment of complete honesty where this man was concerned, she was forced to accept that she had little or no resistance against him.

While his tongue ravaged her mouth, his hands moved down her back, finding every sensitive nub of her spine, curving over her bottom, bringing her intimately close to his hard body. Like her, he was fully aroused, and she kicked off her sandals to stand on her toes and fit herself more satisfactorily to his throbbing maleness.

For a few moments, she lost total control. The fact that they were standing on the deck of his yacht, in full view of anyone who chose to walk along the dock, was forgotten. The way he was kissing her, the way he was caressing her, the way he was rubbing his hips against hers, drove all sane thoughts out of her head. She just wanted him to go on proving that she was still a desirable, sensuous woman, and only when she felt his hand slide beneath the hem of her skirt did she find the sense to drag herself away from him.

'For pity's sake,' she choked, her trembling hands smoothing her skirt back into place, and she saw by the stunned look in Raul's eyes that he too had been unaware of his surroundings.

'I'm sorry,' he muttered, a faint colour invading his cheeks as his eyes followed hers to the evidence of the erection he was unable to hide. 'God!' He turned abruptly away. 'You must think I'm an animal.'

Ally drew a trembling breath. 'Not—not that,' she said huskily, and then turned to grip the rail behind her. 'Do you want me to go back?'

'You *know* what I want and that's not it,' he said in a low impassioned voice. Then, as if he couldn't stand to continue with that conversation, he said crisply, 'Welcome aboard the *Isabella*. She was named for my mother.' He paused, before adding steadily, 'I'll cast off. We're wasting the best of the day.'

Ally turned in his direction again but he wasn't looking her way. Instead, he'd gone ashore to release the mooring lines, and, as she watched, he shoved the gangway aside and vaulted back on board. For a few moments, she was completely absorbed with what he was doing and she gazed at him helplessly, her heart in her eyes. Oh, God, she wasn't falling in love with him, was she? she asked herself despairingly. That really would be stupid.

Yet there was no denying that she'd never experienced anything like the emotions Raul could inspire in her. And she was very much afraid that he was in danger of destroying much more than her self-respect...

It was after two o'clock when Raul again tied up the *Isabella* at her mooring.

It was much later than Ally had anticipated, though she acknowledged that she ought to have been prepared for it when Raul had produced the picnic basket from the boot of the car.

But then, that had been before she'd made such a fool of herself on the jetty. Since that incident, and its subsequent aftermath, there'd been a certain surreal quality to the day. Whatever she'd thought there was between them had been banished as completely as the sun on a rainy afternoon and she was no longer sure of anything—least of all what he thought of her.

Yet, Raul had behaved as if nothing untoward had happened. Well, not quite that, she acknowledged wryly. But he hadn't referred to that scene on the deck of the *Isabella* again and Ally had been left with the uneasy feeling that perhaps she'd only imagined the hunger in his voice.

Still, on a purely objective level, she supposed the day had been a success. Raul had handled the large yacht with enviable ease, proving that he hadn't been exaggerating when he'd told her how he used to spend his summers as a boy. He'd used the yacht's engines to steer the boat out of the marina and then hoisted the sails, allowing the warm wind to fill them.

To someone who'd never sailed before, the sheer delight of skimming though the foam-flecked waves, of competing with the birds and sea creatures in their own element, had been magical. Ally knew she could never satisfactorily express her gratitude at being given this opportunity, and she hoped Raul understood how she felt.

But since he'd kissed her, since she'd practically begged him to let her go, their relationship had changed in some fundamental way and Ally didn't know how to retrieve it. She wanted to tell him that he hadn't offended her, that she didn't think he was an animal or anything like that, but she didn't know how. It was as if the man she'd known had disappeared and in his place was someone she felt she hardly knew at all. The idea of approaching something so—personal—with this stranger was too daunting to contemplate and for the past few hours they'd maintained a polite detachment that was as unfamiliar as it was uncomfortable.

Not that Raul had stopped speaking to her altogether. On the contrary, he'd spent some time pointing out places of interest along the coast, drawing her attention to different rock formations, even discussing the chances of finding the wreck of a treasure ship among the rocks and coral reefs that studded these waters. Almost like a professional guide, she reflected bitterly, sure he was wishing he'd never suggested taking her out.

They'd had lunch at one o'clock, anchored off a deserted cove that looked to be totally untouched. Indeed, Ally had wondered if anyone had ever set foot on its unspoilt beach, although as Raul had known it was here that had probably been a naïve thought.

Nevertheless, she had been absurdly tempted when he'd suggested that if she'd like to go for a swim there was no doubt a swimsuit she could use in the cabin below. But the thought of appearing before him in the kind of scanty outfit a much slimmer woman might wear had been too depressing to consider, and it was only now that she speculated whether she hadn't spurned the best chance of reaching him that she'd had.

Whatever, she'd heard the unmistakable splash as he'd gone into the water, and it had taken an immense effort of will to stay where she was and not go rushing to the rail to watch him.

Now, however, they were back at the marina with nothing resolved between them and Ally decided it was probably just as well. Their relationship had had no future, after all, and it was possible that he had realised it, too.

# CHAPTER TEN

ALLY was standing by the gangway when Raul came back on board.

She hadn't made the mistake of putting her sandals on again. They could wait until she was safely back on the quay. Cursing the slightly breathy note in her voice, she said, 'Are you ready?'

'As I'll ever be,' remarked Raul drily, regarding her with quizzical eyes. 'The question is, are you?'

'Me?' Ally's voice rose an octave and she made an effort to control it. 'Of course. Why not?'

'Have you forgiven me for embarrassing you earlier?'

'For—for embarrassing me?' Ally swallowed. 'I'm not sure I know what you mean.'

'Oh, I think you do.' Raul's nostrils flared for a moment. 'Despite what you think of me, I'm not usually in the habit of attempting to seduce my—companion, date, call it what you will—in full view of anyone who cares to look.'

Ally shook her head. 'It doesn't matter—'

'It does matter.' When she would have moved past him, he blocked her way. 'Don't pretend you don't know what I'm talking about. Why else have you treated me like a stranger for the past four hours?'

Ally stared at him. '*I've* treated *you* like a stranger?' She made a defensive sound. 'I've only taken my cue from you.'

'From me?' He seemed genuinely taken aback. He raked long fingers through the wind-tumbled darkness of his hair. 'How was I suppose to act, for God's sake? You've made it perfectly clear, on more than one occasion now, that my behaviour disgusts you. Well, guess what? Today I've disgusted myself, too.'

Ally moistened her lips. 'I think we'd better go,' she said hastily. 'Suzanne will be wondering where we are. I'm sure she didn't realise we were going to be out so long. But— but I do appreciate your giving me this opportunity to experience sailing first-hand. It's been—wonderful!'

Raul's lips twisted. 'Has it?'

'Well, for me it has,' said Ally firmly, stepping round him. 'Even if I've ruined everything?'

Ally gained the comparative security of the dock before glancing back over her shoulder. 'There was nothing to ruin,' she told him, with a nervous little shake of her head. 'Um—are you coming?'

Raul scowled, but he obediently collected the picnic basket and followed her along the planked walk back to the quay.

The sun was still very hot and Ally was aware that, despite her efforts to stay in the shade of the yacht's awning, her arms and her calves were itching with the heat. She dreaded to think what her face must look like and she curled into her seat with her head turned resolutely away from him when he climbed into the car beside her.

They seemed to get back to the hotel in record time and Ally guessed that Raul had chosen to concentrate all his energies on his driving and not on her. Which was just as well, she acknowledged, dry-mouthed. She didn't know how much longer she could maintain a façade of indifference when every nerve in her body was crying out for his touch.

He brought the convertible to a halt at the foot of the steps where he'd picked her up that morning. But before she could open her door and escape into the hotel, his hand closed possessively on her thigh.

'I'm sorry,' he said, his low voice disturbing her almost as much as his hand on her hot flesh. 'I don't know what came over me. If it's any compensation, I have to say that you seem to bring out the worst in me.'

'Then—then it's just as well that we won't be seeing one

another again,' Ally declared unsteadily, her breath catching in her throat. She put her hand over his in an attempt to get him to remove it and, when he met her efforts with obvious resistance, she met his sensual gaze with a challenging look. 'You don't want to—to repeat the offence, do you?'

She thought he was going to argue with her. Then, with a muttered oath, he withdrew his hand. However, her relief was short-lived. 'We will be seeing one another again,' he said, and Ally hoped she was only imagining the grim determination in his words. 'Tomorrow night at Finisterre.' He flung himself back in his seat. 'Be there.'

How Ally got up the steps and into the hotel, she never knew. Her legs were so shaky she wasn't totally convinced that they'd support her, and the awareness of Raul's eyes upon her—upon the curve of her bottom and thighs, she reminded herself uneasily, smoothing her skirt down over her hips as best she could—was an added impediment.

But somehow she made it into the hotel, only to come face to face with Julia in the lobby.

'So there you are.' Julia's tone was decidedly peevish and Ally hoped she was not going to have to face a confrontation with her. But the girl only looked beyond her and demanded querulously, 'Where's Raul?'

'I—oh—he's gone, I think.' In all honesty, Ally didn't know where Raul was at this moment, and she told herself she didn't want to know.

'Gone?' Julia's attention transferred itself back to her. 'Oh, Aunt Ally, don't say you didn't invite him in.'

Ally gave an inward groan, but, before she was obliged to make some response, Suzanne came out of the dining room and smiled when she saw her friend.

'Ally,' she exclaimed. 'You look as if you've had a good time.'

'Do I?' Ally wasn't at all convinced that her appearance warranted such an interpretation but she was only too willing to agree if it meant avoiding an argument with Julia

'Actually, I can't wait to get in the shower.' She fanned herself theatrically. 'It's been so hot.'

'I can see that.' Suzanne didn't sound quite so sympathetic now. 'You should have borrowed a hat.'

'Raul's gone, Mum.'

Before Ally could say anything else, Julia intervened, and although her tone was laconic, Suzanne immediately glanced round the foyer. 'He has?' she exclaimed anxiously, and Ally realised that it was Suzanne and not her daughter who looked the most perturbed. Her eyes flicked back to Ally. 'Where is he? Didn't he bring you back?'

Ally wanted to groan aloud. 'Well, yes,' she said evenly, 'but I suppose he thought that as he's—seeing you all tomorrow evening…'

She let her voice trail away, hoping they'd accept what she was trying to say, but Suzanne still looked troubled. 'It's not like Raul to leave without saying goodbye,' she said, her brows drawing together in a frown. 'Everything was all right, wasn't it? You haven't fallen out with him or anything? After what I told you—'

'Oh, come on, Mum.' Julia made an impatient gesture now. 'Aunt Ally's probably right. You know what his mother's like. I bet she told him to get back in good time to help her. After all, he has been out of her sight for a good five hours!'

'I wish you wouldn't be so sarcastic, Julia.' Her mother gave her a reproving stare. 'Just because Isabel relies on Raul is no reason to make fun of her. Don't forget, she's had a lot to contend with in her life.'

'Yeah, right.' Julia was sardonic. 'It must have been real tough marrying a millionaire and living at Finisterre all these years. My heart bleeds for her.'

'Julia!' Suzanne was angry now. 'I won't have you speaking of your future mother-in-law in that way. You know very well that she's been in and out of hospital for the past twelve

months. The woman's had cancer, for goodness sake! Surely
you don't begrudge her the time she spends with her son.'

'She does have more than one son,' retorted Julia sulkily.
'I don't see Carlos running after her like Raul does.'

'That's because that young man is as selfish as you are,'
declared Suzanne in a low impatient tone. 'Now, if that's
all you've got to say, I suggest you go and help your father.
He's in the cellar with José, checking the wine stocks.'

The girl made a horrified sound. 'But I've just had my
hair done,' she protested.

'So?'

Suzanne arched an imperious brow and, with a gesture of
disgust, Julia flounced away. But when Ally would have
followed her, Suzanne put a hand on her arm to detain her.

'I'd like to have word with you, Ally,' she said, renewing
all Ally's earlier apprehension. 'I think you have something
to tell me, don't you?'


Ally decided to go for a walk after dinner that evening. She
wasn't in the mood to go to bed and spend the next couple
of hours fretting over what had happened that morning and,
equally, she had no desire to discuss it with anyone else.
Particularly Suzanne, who was obviously more concerned
with what she was going to do about Jeff.

Jeff.

Ally took a deep breath and kicked off her sandals as she
stepped down onto the beach. That was what Suzanne had
wanted to talk to her about earlier. Sam had rung while she
was out with Raul and her daughter had had no hesitation
about telling Suzanne exactly what was going on at home.
She'd assumed her mother would have confided in her friend
and that was why Suzanne had sounded so offended when
she'd told Ally that she wanted to speak to her. She'd
wanted to know how Ally felt about it and why she'd kept
the news to herself.

Unfortunately, Ally had been so relieved that her friend

hadn't discovered anything about herself and Raul that she'd been far more expansive about her feelings than she should have been. She'd left the other woman in no doubt that she didn't want a reconciliation with Jeff, and in consequence any chance of using that as a reason for returning to England had been stymied.

Naturally Suzanne had supported her decision. 'The man's a louse,' she'd declared, squeezing Ally's shoulder in a gesture of encouragement. 'Even Samantha agrees with me. I suggest you ignore anything he might say to the children to get their sympathy and be glad you're not there to pick up the pieces.'

*To pick up the pieces.*

Suzanne's words came back to haunt her. Was that how her friend saw Jeff's situation? Despite the way he'd treated her, Ally knew she wouldn't be happy thinking that her ex-husband was falling apart. He was Sam and Ryan's father, after all. That should afford him some respect.

She sighed. She didn't want to think about Jeff now. Maybe in the morning she'd give the matter some serious consideration. For tonight she just wanted to escape her problems—most of which she'd brought upon herself, she conceded unhappily—and enjoy the warm wind in her hair and the distinctive scent of the ocean breaking on the sand just a few feet away.

She had left the lights that illuminated the steps behind and was just thinking that perhaps she ought to be turning back when she sensed she was no longer alone. It wasn't that she had actually heard someone behind her, but rather an awareness of their presence, of other lungs breathing the soft warm air.

She felt a twinge of panic. Had someone—some man, perhaps—seen her leave the grounds of the hotel and decided to follow her? Had he followed her down the steps, keeping at a safe distance until he'd estimated that he couldn't be heard from above?

There was only one way to find out. Telling herself that she was probably imagining it—or, if not, that it could be anyone, even Tom Adams—Ally glanced apprehensively over her shoulder.

Her lips parted in dismay. Not Tom Adams, she acknowledged tensely, taking a deep breath as she turned to face her pursuer. 'What are you doing here?'

'Following you. What else?' asked Raul drily, slipping his hands into the pockets of his silk trousers as he came nearer. 'You shouldn't be out here alone, you know. It's not wise.'

'Because I might be accosted?' asked Ally wryly. 'Oh, right. You just proved it.'

'You don't have to be afraid of me, Ally,' retorted Raul, with some heat. 'I thought we dealt with that this morning. I've said I'm sorry. I don't see what more I can do.'

'How about keep away from me?' suggested Ally, aware that she wasn't handling this at all well. She had hoped to achieve some kind of detachment before she saw Raul again, but the circumstances of this meeting had seriously damaged what little self-possession she had.

'You know I can't do that,' he said now, turning to stare broodingly at the horizon. There was a moon, but its light was fleeting as it dodged the clouds that were massing over the headland. 'I didn't intend to come here tonight. When I left home I had no clear notion of where I was going.'

'So you came here.'

'Yes.'

'To see Julia?'

'No, not to see Julia,' he said harshly. 'I came to see you. Can't you understand? I wanted to be with you. I wasn't convinced you'd believed me this morning, and I see now I was right.'

Ally tugged her lower lip between her teeth. The temptation to look at him without his being aware of it was irresistible, however, and, although she knew it was crazy, she couldn't drag her eyes away.

He was dressed all in black this evening: a black silk shirt and loose-fitting trousers that billowed against his strong muscular legs. She knew what those legs felt like against hers, she thought, almost incredulously; knew the fine dark hair that arrowed down his chest; had felt how it coarsened to protect the dormant power of his sex...

Oh, God!

With a swift intake of breath she forced herself to look away, and as she did so she realised she was wasting her opportunity to get away from him. If he followed her back to the hotel, then so be it. She would feel far safer in the brightly lit environs of the lobby, even if her fears were more to do with her weaknesses than his.

'You made it easy for me,' he said, before she could move away from him, and his words arrested her.

'I beg your pardon?' she began, and he turned to give her a weary look.

'By coming down here,' he said flatly. 'What did you think I meant? You haven't made anything else easy. And it was just luck that I happened to see you leaving the hotel.'

'Luck?'

Ally tried to sound sarcastic and failed abysmally. But she couldn't deny that the things he was saying scared her. Their relationship had never been meant to be like this.

She had to leave, but when she started past him, he spoke again. 'Don't go,' he said softly. 'Please.'

Ally couldn't look at him now. 'I must.'

'Why?'

*Why?* He asked her that? 'You know why,' she said in a muffled voice. 'You shouldn't even be here.'

'I know why you think you have to go, but you're mistaken,' he replied huskily. 'What are we doing that's so wrong? I'm not touching you, am I? I'm not forcing you to touch me?'

'But you want to,' she said, her voice strangled, and his acknowledgement was faintly ironic.

'Well, yes,' he said. 'But it's what we both want. You just don't like to admit it.'

Ally stifled a sob. 'That's not true.'

'Of course it's true.' He was almost dismissive. 'We were meant to be together. Standing there, so fiercely indignant in your demure little dress. You want me just as much as I want you, Ally. When are you going to recognise that fact?'

'Never.'

Shivering, Ally wrapped her arms about her waist. It was a form of protection, only she knew she had no real protection from him. Yes, she wanted him, she acknowledged. How could she not? He was the only man she had ever...

She stopped herself there; stopped short of the ultimate admission. No, she told herself angrily. She didn't love him. She *couldn't* love him. That way lay disaster—for everyone.

'I'm going back,' she insisted unsteadily, trying not to notice how the moonlight tinged his dark hair with silver, accentuated the aquiline lines of his face. He looked tired, she thought, but that was not her problem. 'It's getting late.'

His shrug was indifferent. 'If you must,' he said carelessly. 'Me: I'm going for a swim.'

Ally gazed at him in dismay now. 'You can't,' she exclaimed, as his hands went to the buckle of his belt. 'I mean...' She shook her head disbelievingly. 'You can't mean you're going to swim in your—your underwear?'

'I'm not wearing any underwear,' he replied, unbuttoning his shirt, and her mouth went wide when he dropped his trousers onto the sand.

It was true. He wasn't wearing any underwear. He was completely naked beneath the folds of black silk. And, evidently uncaring of what she thought of him—of what she did—he turned and strode purposefully into the water.

She should leave. She knew that. Knew it with a certainty that bordered on hysteria. But she didn't go. On legs that felt decidedly unsteady, she moved closer to the ocean, catching her breath when he waded out until the waves were lapping his waist before diving headlong into the water.

Dear heaven!

Pressing the tips of her fingers together against her lips, Ally stared at the place where he had disappeared. Her eyes were glued to the spot, and she watched with dry-mouthed intensity until a glossy dark head broke the surface. She'd been afraid, so afraid...

Breathing fitfully, she watched as he swam away from the shore, treading into the shallows herself when she feared he didn't intend to come back. She had no idea what she'd have done if he'd continued outward. She could swim, but she doubted her strength would be sufficient against the tide. But he did turn back and she staggered unsteadily onto the beach again, aware that the hem of her skirt was now soaked with salt water.

'Why don't you join me?' he called, when he was near enough for her to hear him, but all Ally could do was shake her head.

'I don't think so,' she said, hardly aware that she had picked up his shirt and trousers and was cradling them against her chest. 'You should come out.'

'Why?' He was tormenting her, she realised, but there was nothing she could do to stop him. 'I've got nothing better to do,' he added. 'You won't talk to me, so—'

'I'm sure Julia would be only too happy to see you,' said Ally swiftly. 'Besides, you'll get cold, and you've got no towel to dry yourself.'

'The water's warm,' he assured her. 'But it pleases me that you should care about my health. Perhaps all is not lost, after all.' His voice gentled. 'Join me.'

Ally shook her head again, turning away. 'Oh, God, Raul,' she whispered to herself, pressing her face into the soft fabric of his shirt, and then almost jumped out of her skin when strong arms slipped about her waist from behind.

'Oh, God, Raul—what?' he asked, uncaring that his wet body was dampening her dress. He pressed himself against her and she could feel his instantaneous reaction. 'Stop fighting me, Ally. I need you. We need each other.'

'*No!*'

With a tortured cry, Ally came to her senses, the senses that had been momentarily seduced into an involuntary surrender. With his clothes tumbling unheeded from her hands, she tore herself away from him, running back along the beach as if the devil himself—or the temptation he offered—was at her heels.

# CHAPTER ELEVEN

SUZANNE had told her that a car was coming to pick them up at seven o'clock the following evening and, by a quarter to the hour, Ally was in a fine state of nerves.

She'd spent the last few hours selecting and discarding every item in her limited wardrobe and although she'd finally decided on the black dress she'd worn at the hotel in London, she wasn't happy about it. It brought back too many memories, most of them unwelcome, and she hoped Raul wouldn't think she'd worn the dress deliberately to remind him of their first meeting.

Her lips compressed as she viewed her reflection in the mirror. Of course he wouldn't, she decided painfully. She doubted if he found anything about her particularly memorable. He was sexually attracted to her. She'd been forced to accept that. However unlikely it seemed when they were apart, it was true, but she had no delusions that he wanted any more than he had had already.

And yet, the night before...

But she didn't want to think about the night before. She didn't understand what had happened. She only knew she had spent the rest of the night and all day today trying to put it out of her head.

He didn't care, she told herself fiercely. He enjoyed teasing her and making love with her, but she would only be fooling herself if she expected anything more of him. He was going to marry Julia; he *had* to marry Julia. And she was simply his final bid for sexual freedom.

Whatever, she had no more time to think about their relationship now. Not that it was a relationship, really. It was just a rather tawdry affair that she should have known better

than to get involved in. It wasn't as if she was any good at
relationships, tawdry or otherwise. The years she'd spent
with Jeff should have taught her that. And she was only
building up a store of trouble for herself by allowing it to
go on.

Downstairs, Peter, Suzanne and Julia were waiting for her.
Ally thought how dowdy she must appear compared to their
colourful sophistication. But the women were wearing what
even Ally recognised were designer gowns, and she guessed
this was one occasion when money was considered no object.

'You look nice,' said Suzanne at once, tucking her arm
through Ally's, and Ally wondered if that was what they
meant by being damned with faint praise.

'So do you,' she said sincerely, admiring the other
woman's ankle-length taffeta. 'That shade of blue really
suits you.'

'Oh, do you think so?' Suzanne was evidently pleased.
'Well, I had to have something decent for this evening.' She
lowered her voice. 'Don't say anything, but I think Julia's
hoping that Raul will pop the long-awaited question tonight.'
She squeezed Ally's arm. 'Exciting, isn't it?'

'Very,' Ally managed, aware of a certain tightness in her
chest. She glanced nervously about the foyer. 'Is the car here
yet?'

'This looks like it now,' declared Peter, stepping forward
as a uniformed chauffeur came though the swing doors.
'Shall we go, ladies?'

Julia took her father's arm as they all left the hotel and
descended the steps to where a long black limousine was
waiting. The three women got in the back and Peter climbed
into the front beside the driver. Then they were off, moving
smoothly down the drive and out onto the same road that
Ally and Raul had taken yesterday morning.

'It's good of the Ramirezes to send a car for us,' remarked
Suzanne happily, totally unaware of Ally's tension. 'It

means Pete can have a drink without worrying about having to drive home.'

'Well, I think Raul could have come for us himself,' said Julia somewhat petulantly. 'Or Carlos, at least. We are almost family, after all.'

'"Almost" being the operative word,' observed her mother, with a worried glance towards the chauffeur. Then, changing the subject, 'Do you like Julia's dress, Ally? It's by a top designer.'

'Oh—yes.' Ally forced herself to look at the younger woman. Even in the shadowy light of the car the folds of coral-coloured fabric that draped the girl's breasts were visible. 'It's beautiful. Is it silk?'

'What else?' asked Julia smugly, fingering the neckline of the dress. 'I intend to get used to clothes like this.'

'Julia!'

Once again her mother cast her an impatient look and Ally tried very hard not to care. But she couldn't help wondering if Raul had any idea how mercenary his future wife was or whether Julia cared more for the man or the financial security he represented.

The route to Finisterre wound across the island, the moonlight glinting on the insignia on the bonnet of the limousine. As they left the busier area to the east of the island behind them, the road seemed to get narrower, or perhaps it was just the density of the vegetation that crowded in on either side of the car.

From time to time Ally caught a glimpse of the ocean encroaching on the sands at the foot of rocky cliffs. Less frequently, she saw the moon sailing above them, its silvery light throwing the faces of her friends into sharp relief.

She tried not to be apprehensive, but it was almost impossible, and she knew a feeling of disbelief at being here at all. What was she doing? she wondered. She didn't belong in this company. She was an ordinary housewife, not a wannabe socialite like Julia and Suzanne.

Nevertheless, when they reached the Ramirez estate, she couldn't deny the feeling of excitement that gripped her. Her first sight of Raul's home was a memorable one and, in spite of the misgivings that had tormented her for much of the journey, she found herself moving forward in her seat, gazing out of the limousine's window with wide enquiring eyes.

She'd known they were on Ramirez land for some time, but nothing had prepared her for the beauty of it all. The abundant vegetation had given way to white-railed paddocks where the occasional gleam of a polished coat or the flash of a silvery mane betrayed the presence of horses. Thoroughbreds, probably, she reflected, wondering if Raul and Julia went riding together. It was the sort of thing they might do: like sailing, it was a wealthy man's pursuit.

Beyond the paddocks, walls overgrown with bougainvillaea hid gardens filled with roses and night-scented blossoms that enveloped the car in their fragrance. A hedge of scarlet hibiscus guarded the inevitable swimming pool that was floodlit from below the water, and they turned into a lamplit courtyard where tubs of geraniums provided vivid splashes of colour.

'Magnificent, isn't it?' murmured Suzanne smugly, evidently pleased by Ally's reaction. 'Wait until you see the house.'

Ally was tempted to say that she could already see the house, but she guessed the white walls of the graceful plantation-style dwelling that confronted them hid a wealth of elegant features. The wide wrap-around verandah, that supported the iron-railed balconies above on tall marble columns, was some indication of how impressive the interior must be, and when Peter opened the door for his wife to get out, Ally followed on slightly uncertain legs.

The chauffeur had opened the other door for Julia and she came round the car to join them as a uniformed butler came out of the house to welcome them. With the muted roar of the sea echoing in Ally's ears, they were escorted up the shallow verandah steps and through double doors into a high-ceilinged reception hall. A glittering chandelier hung at the curve of a sweeping staircase, its light glinting on the tiered fountain that sparkled in the middle of the marble floor. Huge urns of orchids sheltered in the well of the stairs, while the delicate bronze of a dancer adorned one of the many niches that illuminated the walls. The feeling was one of light and colour, and Ally found it almost impossible to take it in.

'What did I tell you?' whispered Suzanne, as a tall distinguished-looking man appeared in the sculpted archway to their right. He paused, smiled, and then came to meet them, his aquiline features so like his son's that Ally knew immediately who he was.

'Suzanne, Peter, Julia,' he said smoothly, shaking Peter's hand and raising Suzanne's almost to his lips in continental fashion. Julia chose to step forward and kiss her future father-in-law on both cheeks, and Ally had the impression that Juan Ramirez would have preferred a less familiar salutation. However, his tone was warm as he continued, 'I am pleased you could come.'

'It's our pleasure,' declared Suzanne effusively and Peter echoed her words. Then, drawing Ally forward, she said, 'May I introduce my old friend Alison Sloan?'

'Mrs Sloan.' Raul's father turned to her with obvious pleasure. 'I am delighted to meet you at last.' He took her hand between both of his, holding it rather longer than was necessary, Ally was sure. He studied her intently. 'My wife has been ill, you understand? In consequence, our earlier invitation had to be postponed.'

'I understand.' Ally didn't know what to say and she was aware that the Davises were watching them with curious eyes. There was also a certain amount of resentment—on Julia's part, at least—and, drawing her hand away, she murmured, 'I hope Señora Ramirez is feeling much better this evening.'

'Oh, she is. Much better,' he assured her, releasing her hand with some reluctance. He held out his arm. 'Come.' He included the others in the invitation. 'Isabel is waiting for us on the patio. I thought we might have pre-dinner drinks outdoors, if that is acceptable.'

Ally hardly noticed the elegant dining room they passed through on their way to the floodlit patio. She had a swift impression of another high-ceilinged room with gleaming dark furniture around a candlelit table, but she was so self-conscious at being singled out for attention she found it difficult to concentrate on anything else. Conscious, too, of the Davises following behind, and of what she suspected was Suzanne's resentment at being ignored.

'Where's Raul?' demanded Julia, displaying her pique in the sulkiness of her voice, but Juan Ramirez was unperturbed.

'Rafael will join us shortly,' he said as they emerged onto a paved terrace where the sound of the sea was louder. Several comfortable cane chairs and loungers were set beneath a fluttering awning. 'Here we are, Isabel. Our guests have arrived.'

A refrigerated drinks trolley, attended by a white-coated waiter, was standing to one side, but Ally's eyes were instantly drawn to the dark-haired woman who was rising with some difficulty from a cushioned rocker. She was so pale, and excessively thin, and Ally desperately wanted to rush towards her and assure her that she had no need to get up for them.

But etiquette dictated that she do nothing of the kind and there was no doubt that there was pride and hauteur in every line of Isabel Ramirez's narrow face. There was beauty, too, Ally realised; the kind of beauty that had shown itself in the sensual curve of Raul's mouth and the night-dark intensity of his eyes. He was, without doubt, a unique blend of both his parents and her mouth dried at the thought of meeting him again in their company.

'Isabel!' Clearly not prepared to be relegated to a supporting role on this occasion, Suzanne went swiftly past Juan and her friend to take Isabel Ramirez's hands in both of hers. 'It's so wonderful to see you again. How are you feeling? We've been so worried about you.'

Had they? Ally tried not to remember that Isabel's illness had only been mentioned in the most disparaging way between Suzanne and her daughter, and she was hardly surprised when Raul's mother deflected any attempt to patronise her.

'I assure you, I am feeling much better, Suzanne,' she assured her coolly. 'How are you? I seem to remember Julia telling us that you have been plagued by headaches in recent weeks. I trust it is nothing serious. Have you consulted with Dr Carrington, perhaps?'

Suzanne cast her daughter an impatient look. 'Julia exaggerates,' she said stiffly, and Ally guessed the girl had not heard the last of that. 'I'm perfectly all right.'

'That is good—'

'This is Mrs Sloan, *querida*.' With admirable skill, Juan Ramirez interposed himself between his wife and Suzanne, causing Ally no little embarrassment in the process. 'You recall, Rafael was speaking of her earlier?'

'Oh, yes. Of course.' As Ally speculated on what Raul could have been telling his parents about her, Isabel Ramirez held out a slim elegant hand. 'Welcome to Finisterre, Mrs Sloan. I am so glad you were able to accept our invitation.'

'I—' Ally glanced awkwardly at Suzanne who was regarding her with unconcealed irritation now. 'It was kind of you to invite me. But, please—call me Ally, won't you?'

'Yes, and I'd like to say how much we appreciated Raul—Rafael—taking Ally sailing yesterday morning,' put in Suzanne, determined not to be outdone. 'It was very good of him.'

Isabel's lips twitched, and she arched an aristocratic brow

at her husband. 'I doubt if Rafael invited Mrs—*Ally*—to go sailing out of the goodness of his heart,' she remarked drily. And Ally, who had been smarting a little at her friend's attempt to make her feel small, wasn't the only one who wondered what she meant. Isabel's eyes moved past them then, and a smile brought real beauty to her olive-skinned features. 'Here he is now. Perhaps we should ask him.'

# CHAPTER TWELVE

ALLY stifled a yawn and suppressed the urge to prop her elbow on the table to support her head on her fist. The headache, which had appeared without warning a couple of hours ago, was probably due to the amount of wine she'd consumed, she thought gloomily, though watching Suzanne trying to ingratiate herself with Juan and Isabel Ramirez might have had something to do with it. This was a side of her friend she'd never seen before and if it hadn't been so embarrassing it would have been pathetic.

Of course, her headache had nothing to do with the fact that since Raul had joined them, Julia had monopolised his attention. That was as it should be, she told herself severely, despising the curling snake of jealousy that was twisting in her belly. Who knew but that if she hadn't become involved with Raul, he and Julia might have been engaged by now? She was crazy to think that just because his mother and father had been kind to her she meant anything to him. Indeed, apart from a few perfunctory words on his arrival, he'd hardly spoken to her.

It might have been easier if she hadn't been seated directly opposite him. As it was, she had Carlos, Raul's younger brother—who had probably only been hauled in to even the numbers—on one side, and Suzanne's husband on the other. And, although Peter was a nice man, his conversation did tend to focus on the hotel. Meanwhile Carlos would have obviously preferred to have been seated with Julia, and Ally suspected he found her as boring as she found Peter.

Still, the meal would be over soon, please God. She'd already lost count of the number of courses they'd been offered and despite the fact that many of them had been little more than appetisers served between the main dishes, Ally had found some of the food a little rich for her taste. Stuffed olives, marinated anchovies, spicy fried fish: delicious, perhaps, but when they were served before courses of sautéed chicken and a Bahamian version of paella, they were just too much.

Or perhaps it was her fault, Ally thought wearily. There was no doubt that without emotional pressures she would have welcomed the opportunity to try this mixture of Spanish and Bahamian cuisine, and maybe if she hadn't drunk so much rich red burgundy she would not be feeling so miserable now.

She'd refused to have any of the exotic desserts that had been offered before coffee. Thick creamy custards and sweet *tortillas*; peaches cooked in rum-flavoured syrup and sugary pastries, were not to her taste at any time, but particularly not this evening. However, both Julia and Suzanne made up for her tardiness, the latter complimenting her hostess several times on the superb quality of the ingredients. Ally thought, rather unkindly, that, although her mother was slim, Julia would have to be careful about her weight. She was already a little plump, and as she got older...

But Ally stopped herself right there. For heaven's sake, who was she to talk? She was letting her feelings for Raul influence every aspect of her life and she had to stop it. However long she decided to prolong this agony, sooner or later she would have to go back to England, and it was the problems that she faced there that should be occupying her thoughts now.

'Should we have coffee on the patio?' suggested Isabel a few moments later and as there seemed to be general agreement around the table Ally got eagerly to her feet. Although the room was air-conditioned, she couldn't wait to breathe some clean fresh air, and, surging ahead of the others, she stepped outside.

A low wall topped by a wrought-iron railing formed a

barrier at the far side of the terrace and, drawn by the sound of the ocean, Ally made her way towards it. Gripping the spikes at the top of the railings, she stared out across the moonlit garden and realised that the sea was only about fifty yards from the house.

'Do you like the view?'

Raul's question alerted her to the fact that he had come to stand beside her. In his charcoal silk suit and pale grey shirt he was more formally dressed than she was used to and it was almost impossible to believe that only twenty-four hours ago he had stood naked before her.

How could he? she wondered achingly. How could he be so cool one minute and so passionate the next? Her head was in turmoil and he was behaving as if they were only the slightest of acquaintances when they both knew they were so much more.

Or she knew it, she amended, aware that she was allowing her emotions far too much licence. Why couldn't she accept that what had happened between them meant so much more to her?

'It's very nice,' she replied inadequately now, without looking at him. Not that she needed to, she acknowledged. She'd been sitting opposite him all evening, and, although she'd purposefully avoided his eyes, she was well aware of how attractive he looked. 'I didn't realise we were so close to the sea.'

'Finisterre,' remarked Raul carelessly, propping himself against the rail beside her. 'It's Latin for land's end. I believe there's a story that my great-great-grandfather's mistress named it, but no one really knows.' He paused. 'We like it.'

'I like it, too,' said Ally tightly. 'Who wouldn't? It's beautiful.'

'Thank you.' Raul's tone was sardonic. 'I'll be sure to pass your approval on to my parents.'

Ally gave him a swift look, not quite sure how to take

him, and then, giving a shake of her head, she said, 'Where's your fiancée? Shouldn't you be entertaining her?'

'I don't have a fiancée,' replied Raul flatly. 'And since when have you cared what I do?'

Ally pressed her lips together. His barb had hurt more than he had intended, she was sure, and it took an effort to respond brightly. 'You're right. It isn't anything to do with me. I had no right to offer any opinions where you're concerned.'

'You had every right,' he muttered then, turning to face the railings, his mouth compressed into a thin line. 'And it was my fault. After last night I was sure I could provoke some reaction. Put it down to the fact that I have spent the whole evening wishing we were alone together and now that we are, we're wasting time discussing the name of the house.'

Ally's breath caught in her throat. 'I don't believe you've spent the whole evening wishing we were alone together,' she protested. 'If Julia's attitude was anything to go by, you've certainly convinced her otherwise.'

Raul swore. 'If you're judging my feelings on the strength of Julia's actions, then forget it. My would-be fiancée was behaving as she did for two reasons. One: to annoy my brother. She knows Carlos is crazy about her, and God knows sometimes I think she feels the same way about him. And two: because she has seen how my parents have taken to you, and she does not wish to be—what do you say?— sidelined?'

Ally's eyes widened. 'I don't believe you.'

'It's the truth.'

'But Julia loves you—'

'Does she? I think Julia has an eye to the main chance. Carlos, as you know, is not my father's eldest son.'

Ally's jaw dropped and she hurriedly retrieved it. Then, because she couldn't let this go on, she whispered, 'You shouldn't say such things.'

'Why not?'

'Because—because you're going to marry her.'

'Am I?' His mouth tightened. 'A year ago, my mother developed a breast tumour. It was operable, but her chances at that time were not brilliant and her doctors warned us to anticipate the worst.' He took a deep breath. 'Happily, surgery and radiotherapy performed a minor miracle. She is not cured, but her prognosis is decidedly more optimistic.'

'I see.' Ally didn't know why he was telling her this.

'No, you don't see,' he contradicted her harshly. 'You have to understand that when she was first taken ill, we were all desperate to do anything to make life easier for her. Her greatest wish was to see me married, with children of my own.' He shook his head. 'Until then, I hadn't seriously considered marrying anyone. Selfishly, I suppose, I assumed there was no hurry, and although Julia and I were friends, I had never considered her in that light.'

'So what changed?'

Raul uttered a short mirthless laugh. 'I could be a total jerk and say Julia did, but I have to take the blame for my own actions. She was there, and she was obviously willing and I took advantage of it.'

'You started a relationship?' asked Ally softly, and Raul sighed.

'If you want to call it that.'

'Did your mother and father approve?'

'At that time, I don't think any of us considered that aspect of it. My mother was very ill; dying, maybe. I just wanted to please her.' His lips twisted. 'As they say, it seemed a good idea at the time.'

'It's still a good idea,' she said quickly, remembering what Suzanne had told her. 'I hope you'll be very happy together.'

'No, you don't.' Raul's eyes darkened. 'Goddammit, Ally, I didn't know I was going to meet you when I got involved with Julia. I'd spent twenty-nine years of my life doing pretty much as I pleased, and the idea that some woman might come along and knock the legs out from under me seemed totally unbelievable.'

Ally drew back. 'I don't think we should be having this conversation.'

'Why not?' Raul stared at her. 'Are you going to tell me you don't feel anything for me? Or does the fact that your husband's apparently had a change of heart make a difference? I've been thinking about what you told me. My God, I can think of little else. And, although you insisted you were glad to be out of that relationship, I wonder if that was not all bravado. Perhaps you are still in love with him after all.'

'Perhaps—perhaps—' Ally tried to say Perhaps I am, but the words stuck in her throat. 'However I—however I feel about Jeff,' she said instead, 'that has no bearing on—on your situation.' Her throat was tight as she added fiercely, 'Besides, can you imagine how your mother would feel if you told her what you were doing last night?' Her cheeks filled with shameful colour. 'My God, I'm not convinced your father wouldn't want to throw me out of the house!'

'Why?'

Raul's eyes impaled her, and she shifted helplessly from one foot to the other. 'You know why,' she told him. 'Ours is just—just a sexual relationship. If, indeed, it is any kind of relationship at all.'

'You know better than that,' he said harshly. 'And I am not sure you are right. For me at least—'

'Please.' Ally drew a trembling breath. 'Don't try to make a fool of me. I am not the kind of woman your family needs. You know that. I am too old. I can't promise you the children your mother craves. My children are grown up. They're ready to start families of their own. Can you imagine how they would feel if I told them I was going to start again?'

'Ah, that is the real crux of the matter, isn't it?' said Raul bitterly. 'I think that, whatever you say, you care more about Jeff—about his children—than you do about me.'

*That's not true!*

The words trembled on Ally's tongue, but they were never spoken. Almost instinctively, she sensed that they were no longer alone. Juan Ramirez had come to join them at the balustrade, and she saw Raul thrust his balled fists into his jacket pockets as his father spoke.

'Are you admiring our view, Mrs Sloan?' Juan asked softly, and Ally wondered uneasily if he had known what was going on. 'You must come and see it in daylight. I think I can promise you that it is much more impressive then.'

'I'm sure it is.' Ally knew her palms were sweating and she hastily withdrew them from the railings. Then, seeking something agreeable to say, she appended, 'The sea seems so close.'

'It is.' Juan smiled. 'Which was very convenient for my ancestors. I am sure someone has told you that Rodrigo Ramirez was what we call these days a freebooter. It is a polite way of saying he was a pirate. Isn't that so, Rafael?'

'If you say so, Papá.'

Raul's voice was stiff and Ally was conscious of his father's gaze moving speculatively between them. 'I hope you are not neglecting the civilities, Rafael,' he observed drily. 'Mrs Sloan looks a little distressed. What can you have been saying to her?'

'Nothing of importance, evidently, Papá,' replied Raul politely, squaring his shoulders. 'If you will both excuse me...'

He strode away and Ally forced herself not to look after him. She was very much afraid that, if she did so, her heart would be in her eyes for all to see. But how could she believe that Raul loved her, let alone consider betraying her friend in that way? The situation was impossible. She had to leave.

'My son seems—angry, Mrs Sloan.' Juan watched the younger man go with a frown drawing his greying brows together. 'I must apologise. I cannot think what has got into him.'

Ally blew out a breath. 'I can't imagine,' she lied. Then, because something more was expected of her, she murmured, 'And, please, won't you call me Ally? Mrs Sloan makes me sound so—' She had been about to say old, but she stopped herself. 'So like a stranger.'

'And you are not that, are you, Mrs Sloan?' To her embarrassment, Juan chose not to use the less formal form of address. 'I get the feeling that you and my son know one another rather well. Would I be right in thinking that?'

Ally licked her dry lips. 'I think you should ask him, *señor*,' she murmured unhappily, and he gave her a considering look.

'Perhaps so,' he conceded. 'But I am asking you.' He paused. 'How well do you know Rafael, Mrs Sloan? Rather better than we are aware, I believe.'

Ally shifted uneasily. 'I think you should ask him,' she said again. She hesitated. 'I shouldn't have come here. I realise that now. I hope you'll forgive me for—for abusing your hospitality.'

Juan frowned. 'In what way have you abused my hospitality, Mrs Sloan? My wife and I invited you here.'

'Yes, but—' Ally caught sight of Suzanne watching them from the other side of the patio and stifled a groan. There was no sign of Raul and she thought she could guess what her friend was thinking. 'I—I seem to be in—in everybody's way.'

Juan shrugged. 'You are not in my way, Mrs Sloan. Nor, I would guess, in my wife's. I cannot speak for your friends, of course. They may have their own agenda. But, as far as Rafael is concerned, I got the impression that he wanted rather more than you were prepared to offer.'

Ally's cheeks blazed. '*Señor*—'

'Do not worry, Mrs Sloan. I shall keep my observations to myself. And now, if you will excuse me also, I should attend to my other guests.'

'Of course.'

Ally's voice was choked, and, with a polite gesture, Juan strolled across the patio to where the others were gathered. Coffee had been served and Ally knew she was expected to join them. Suzanne was already angry with her for what had happened earlier. She hadn't said anything, of course, but Ally had known her for too long not to be able to interpret the reason for the coolness in her attitude towards her at dinner. And now, having lured Julia's would-be suitor away from his duties—as Suzanne no doubt perceived it—Ally had had the nerve to sequester Raul's father, too. The glance the other woman had sent in her direction only minutes ago had said it all and Ally was already dreading the ride home.

'Won't you come and join us, Ally?'

Isabel Ramirez apparently had no problem with using her name, and, because she knew it was the best offer she was likely to get, Ally pasted on a smile and walked stiffly back to take the seat Isabel had indicated. 'Thank you.'

'You'll have coffee, yes?' suggested Isabel, summoning the waiter to attend to her guest's needs. 'Were you admiring our view?'

'We were beginning to think that you and the railings were joined at the hip,' put in Suzanne tartly, her words conveying only a fraction of her irritation, Ally was sure. 'For heaven's sake, Ally, what on earth were you and Raul arguing about?'

'Arguing?'

Ally was taken aback. She hadn't been aware that the tone of the discussion she'd been having with Raul was evident, let alone audible. But obviously Suzanne had detected some antagonism between them and she was frantically trying to think of an answer when Juan intervened.

'I think Rafael was offering the opinion that children don't necessarily know what is best for their parents,' he remarked casually. 'You have children, do you not, Ally? Twins, I believe?'

Now how did he know that?

Ally blinked and stared at him with uncomprehending eyes. 'I—yes. Yes, I do,' she agreed, not altogether understanding his meaning. 'A boy and a girl.'

'How wonderful!' It was Isabel who spoke now. 'Do they live with you?'

'Sam—Samantha does,' said Ally, once again conscious of being the cynosure of all eyes. 'Ryan's at university and he shares a flat with—with a friend.'

'With his *girl*friend,' Julia offered smugly. 'Isn't that right, Aunt Ally?'

'And your daughter?' went on Isabel, as if Julia hadn't spoken. 'What does she do?'

'Oh—she's at university, too, but she's able to live at home,' murmured Ally awkwardly. 'But she is planning on getting married next year.'

'Lucky her,' said Julia sulkily. 'It must be nice to feel wanted.'

'You're wanted,' said Carlos at once, and Suzanne gave her daughter a warning look when he stretched out his hand to take Julia's. He grinned, indifferent to her mother's pique. 'Wanna take a walk along the beach?'

'I think it's time we were making a move,' declared Peter quellingly, recognising the look on his wife's face. 'It's been very enjoyable, as always, Isabel. You and Juan must come and have a meal at the hotel.'

'You're very kind.'

Isabel was polite, but Ally sensed such an event was unlikely. As Suzanne had said, there seemed little rapport between the two women.

Suzanne got to her feet. 'You're right,' she said, giving her husband a thin smile. 'We mustn't outstay our welcome.' She glanced about her, as if she'd just noticed that Raul was missing. 'Oh—where's Rafael?'

'Who cares?' muttered Julia sulkily, casting a covetous look at Carlos. 'I don't know why he invited me here. I've hardly spoken to him.'

'Julia!' Suzanne's reproof was automatic. 'You had Raul—*Rafael's* undivided attention all through dinner.' She pulled a wry face at Juan and Isabel, but when her gaze encountered Ally's, a certain maliciousness entered her expression. 'I'm sure he'd rather be spending time with you than entertaining his parents'—other—guests.'

'Perhaps.'

Julia was unconvinced, but Ally, who had been expecting it, was not surprised at Suzanne's unsubtle reference to the conversation she had had with Raul. She was quite sure her friend's hesitation over the word 'other' had been because she had wanted to say 'older' but had chickened out at the last minute.

Raul appeared as they were leaving, and Suzanne was somewhat mollified by his assurance that he'd be seeing Julia again very soon. He barely looked at Ally, but that was all right because she didn't look at him. If he wanted to believe that she still cared about Jeff, so be it, she thought fiercely. It was probably best for all concerned if they didn't see one another again, and perhaps, unwittingly, she had found the ideal way to end it.

# CHAPTER THIRTEEN

BY THE end of the week, Ally had decided that, whatever happened, she had to return to England.

It was not because of anything Suzanne had done. On the contrary, despite a certain coolness towards her on their way back from Finisterre, the other woman had made no further reference to the Ramirezes' dinner party. And, as Raul appeared to have resumed his relationship with Julia, Suzanne seemed content to forget what had happened.

Ally couldn't.

In the days that had followed, she'd found herself more and more on edge, and although she told herself she was glad Raul was staying away from her, the words had a very hollow ring to them.

Which was stupid; she knew that. But, unfortunately, knowing something was true didn't necessarily put an end to it. Just because there was no future in the brief affair— *affair?*—she'd had with Raul, she couldn't forget it. She doubted she ever would and knowing he was with Julia just twisted the knife.

So she'd decided that whatever Suzanne said she'd make Jeff her excuse for going home. And it was true; she was concerned about Sam's attitude towards him. Her daughter had rung her a couple more times during the past few days, and Ally was feeling pretty mean at leaving the whole responsibility for dealing with her father to her.

She had rung Ryan, too, but her son was much more laid back about the situation. As far as he was concerned, he didn't particularly care where his father lived—or with whom. He had his own life to lead, he said, and if Ally thought his reaction smacked a little of Jeff's own, it wasn't something she felt equipped to complain about.

She hadn't spoken to Raul since that night at Finisterre. He had visited the hotel. A couple of times. She'd glimpsed him once, on his own, going into the lift while she was crossing the lobby. But she'd deliberately slowed her steps so that the lift was gone by the time she reached it.

She didn't know how often he'd seen Julia. The girl was often absent, but it was a subject that she considered taboo. Whenever she was with Suzanne or Peter, she carefully avoided anything of a controversial nature. That way, they succeeded in maintaining their friendship, even if it had created a certain distance between them.

However, it was the evening that Mike Mclean came to supper at the hotel that had persuaded Ally that staying here wasn't going to work. She'd almost forgotten that Suzanne had said she would invite the pilot to join them one evening while Ally was there. But, although Ally quite liked the man, she hardly knew him, and his appearance had been another reminder that, as far as Suzanne was concerned, Ally was someone to whom the admiration of a man like Mike Mclean should be flattering.

And it should be, thought Ally unhappily, even though she knew she wasn't attracted to him in that way. She'd been spoilt, she reflected ruefully. She'd tasted heaven and she wanted more. Only that was just a fantasy. Being with Raul was not a choice she was allowed to make.

Nevertheless, the invitation had been an indication that Suzanne hadn't given up on finding her friend an escort while she was on the island. The situation with Tom Adams hadn't worked out, so Suzanne had moved on to her next target.

Maybe she felt more of a need to fix her up with a suitable suitor now, Ally considered wryly. Although Suzanne could have no idea of how well Ally knew her daughter's boyfriend, she had evidently decided that encouraging them to spend time together hadn't been the most sensible thing to do.

Mike Mclean had obviously assumed Ally had encouraged Suzanne to invite him. He'd made a beeline for her and it had been difficult to appear friendly without giving him the wrong impression. It hadn't helped when Suzanne had mentioned that she thought Ally was feeling homesick. That because she and Peter didn't have much time to spend with her, Ally was often left to entertain herself.

In consequence, as he'd been leaving—the Davises had conveniently found something else to do, leaving Ally to see him off—Mike had asked her to go out with him the following evening. Ally had quickly made up a story about agreeing to help Suzanne with her accounts to avoid hurting him, but they had exchanged phone numbers, and Mike had said he would ring in the next couple of days. Which meant she would have to think of something else. If she was still here...

She supposed that was when the idea of leaving really took hold. It would create problems, no doubt, but it would solve a whole lot more. She was tired of deceiving people, tired of living a lie, and even the thought of facing Jeff was more attractive than making excuses to Suzanne as to why she didn't want any more introductions to men her friend thought were eligible. She wasn't available, she thought bitterly. She simply wasn't interested in anyone else.

She tried to speak to Suzanne at breakfast the next morning but her friend was too busy placating a guest, whose air-conditioning wasn't working, to sit down and listen to what Ally had to say. Instead, she promised to free up some time at lunchtime, and Ally had to be content with that.

But, in the event, Raul arrived just before lunch to discuss a business matter with both Davises, and Ally, who had spent the morning on the beach, was more than happy to keep out of the way.

Going up to her room, she took a shower before ordering

a sandwich she didn't particularly want from Room Service, and she was sitting on her balcony, waiting for it to come, when the phone rang.

Despite some misgivings, Ally felt obliged to answer it. It could be Suzanne, after all, she told herself, aware of the prickle of anticipation on her flesh. Just because Raul was in the hotel was no reason to suspect it might be him. On the contrary, he was hardly likely to ring her while he was here.

'H—hello?'

'Mum!' It was Sam, and Ally was glad to sink down onto the side of the bed. 'Mum? Am I glad to reach you. Where have you been?'

'Where have I been?' Ally frowned. 'I haven't been anywhere. I spent the morning on the beach, that's all.' She had thought it might be her last morning and she'd tried to make the most of it. 'Why? What's wrong?'

'Oh, Mum!' Sam made a frustrated sound, and Ally's stomach churned. What could be wrong? 'God, I don't know how to tell you. He's going to arrive shortly. I know, because I phoned the airline and asked what time their flight was due to land in Nassau.'

'Who? Who's going to arrive shortly?' asked Ally anxiously, but she knew. 'Is it your father? Is that what you're saying? Is he on his way out here?'

'Oh, Mum, I tried to stop him. He said he had to speak to you and I said he could do that when you got back. But he wouldn't listen. When I phoned him this morning, his landlady said he'd gone.'

Ally tried to understand what her daughter was saying. 'His landlady?' she echoed, latching on to the last thing Sam had said, and Sam sniffed.

'He moved into a bed-and-breakfast a couple of days ago,' she agreed unhappily. 'I should have known something was going on. He'd been staying at the Post House, but I guess he thought there was no point in paying for a room there when he was planning on going away.'

Ally took a deep breath. 'So he didn't actually tell you he was coming here?'

'Well, he'd talked about it, of course,' admitted Sam ruefully. 'But, like I say, I thought I'd persuaded him to wait until you got back.' She sighed. 'That's why I've been trying to get in touch with you. I wanted to give you some warning. But the receptionist said there was no reply from your room.'

'No.' Ally shook her head a little dazedly. 'No, there wouldn't be. As a matter of fact, I've been thinking of coming home.'

'Because of Dad?' Sam sounded disgusted. 'Oh, Mum!'

'No. Not because of your father,' said Ally firmly. 'Suzanne and me—well, I'm afraid it's not working out.'

'Why?' Sam was dismayed. 'I thought you and she were such good friends.'

'We were. We *are*.' Ally wondered how much to tell her daughter. 'It's just that—well, she thinks I need—male companionship.'

'You do.' Sam was indignant. 'Don't tell me you've turned all prudish in your old age?'

'Excuse me.' Ally was stung by the way her daughter apparently thought of her. 'It's nothing to do with being prudish.' If Sam only knew! 'I just don't need anyone to pick my dates for me.'

'Oh.' Sam sniggered. 'Don't tell me you've been making assignations behind my back.'

'What if I have?' Ally was getting impatient. 'I'm a single woman, aren't I? I don't have to ask your permission to go out with someone other than your father.'

Sam sounded a little less smug now. 'I know,' she said defensively. 'So?' She hesitated. 'Is it anyone I know?'

'What?' Ally swallowed and then, realising she had said

more than she should, she continued, 'No. No one you know. Now, when is your dad due to arrive?'

'Then it's someone you've met while you've been on holiday,' persisted her daughter, clearly unwilling to leave the subject without something more positive to report. 'Who is he? Is he nice? Will I like him? More to the point, is he on holiday, too?'

'Sam!' Ally decided she had said all she was going to on that score. 'We're wasting time. Do you know what time your father is likely to get here?'

'The same time as you did, I suppose,' responded Sam grudgingly. Then, 'You are mean, Mum. If you have met someone, I would have thought I had a right to know.'

Ally groaned. 'Sam, I haven't met anyone. No one important, anyway,' she appended, wishing that were true. 'God, I don't know what Suzanne's going to say when I tell her your father's coming. She may refuse to let him stay.'

'That's not your problem,' retorted Sam, regaining a little of her belligerence. 'I don't suppose Aunt Suzanne's hotel is the only one on the island. He'll have to find somewhere else.'

'Y—e—s.' But Ally was doubtful. If there were other hotels on the island, she didn't know of them, and she doubted Jeff would want to stay at an unlicensed guesthouse. 'Well, we'll see.'

'You won't let him intimidate you, will you, Mum?' Sam sounded anxious now. 'I mean, don't forget he walked out on you, not the other way about. I know he's my father, and I suppose I still love him, but he is a selfish—beggar, isn't he?'

Ally's lips twitched. 'Don't worry, sweetheart,' she said reassuringly. 'I haven't forgotten anything.' She took a breath. 'I'll ring you as soon as I know what I'm doing, right?'

'Right.' But Sam seemed curiously reluctant to hang up. 'Er—Mum?'

Ally tensed. What now? 'Yes?'

'Whoever he is, I hope he makes you happier than Dad ever did.'

Ally realised there was no way she could avoid telling Suzanne that Jeff was likely to turn up in the next few hours. The idea that her ex-husband thought he could interrupt her holiday without even asking her how she felt about it was bad enough, but he must know that Suzanne and Peter didn't like him and would not be best pleased to have him as an uninvited guest.

The sandwich she had ordered from Room Service was still lying untouched on the tray, but a glance at her watch reminded her that she didn't have a lot of time if she wanted to speak to Suzanne before Jeff arrived. Raul must have left the hotel by now, and warning her friend was more important than trying to swallow a sandwich she didn't want any more.

Beige shorts and a cropped tee shirt that just skimmed her waist were the first garments she came to, and, tucking her still damp hair behind her ears, she slipped deck shoes on her feet and left her room. She pressed the button for the lift and waited. It was just on its way down from the upper floor and she breathed a sigh of relief when it stopped at hers.

But when the doors opened, her heart climbed into her throat. Raul was its sole occupant and she had an uneasy sense of *déjà vu*. Like her, he was wearing shorts and deck shoes and a black polo shirt that accentuated the olive cast of his skin. He looked tired, she thought, and the eyes that looked straight into hers revealed a weary resignation.

Ally didn't know what to do. The obvious thing would be to get into the lift with him, but she remembered too well what had happened before and she was wary.

'Are you going down?' he asked flatly, straightening away

from the wall where he'd been lounging. 'Make up your mind.'

Ally's lips tightened. 'I'm going down,' she said, but she still didn't move and a look of irritation crossed Raul's lean face.

'Then get in,' he said, raising a hand to press the button that prevented the doors from closing. 'Or do you want to wait for it to come back up again?'

Ally squared her shoulders. 'That would be stupid.'

'Yes, it would.' Raul agreed with her, and, with some misgivings, Ally stepped inside. The doors closed behind her, as he added, 'But then, you seem to enjoy doing stupid things.'

Ally caught her breath. 'There's no need to be rude about it. If—if you must know, I was wondering if Suzanne was still upstairs in the office.' That wasn't entirely true, but he didn't know that. 'As she said that she and Peter were having a business meeting—'

'I wasn't talking about your hesitation in getting into the lift,' Raul interrupted her shortly. Then, after allowing himself a disturbing appraisal of her upper body, he looked away. 'Ground floor?'

Ally tried to control her breathing. 'Yes,' she said, a little breathlessly. 'The ground floor. Thank you.'

Raul shrugged and resumed his position against the wall of the lift and it continued downward. But the atmosphere in the small cubicle was tense and Ally knew she had to do something to try and ease it.

'How is your mother?' she asked, choosing what she thought was the least controversial of topics, and his dark eyes flicked her way.

'Do you care?'

'Of course I care.' Ally was stung. 'I—I liked her. And I liked your father.'

'Oh, yes. My father.' Raul's voice was sardonic. 'I

understand you and he had quite a conversation after I left the party.'

'We—spoke together, yes.'

'And did you tell him what we'd been talking about?'

'I don't think so.'

'Did you tell him how I felt about you?'

'No!' Ally was horrified now. Then, realising how her words could be misconstrued, she added, 'I don't think you know how you feel about me, let alone anyone else.' The lift shuddered as it reached its destination. 'Oh, we're here.'

'Wait!' Raul followed her out of the lift and she was forced to turn and face him or risk him trailing her across the lobby. 'I do know how I feel about you,' he told her harshly. 'I'd just like to know how you feel about me.'

Ally glanced about her. 'Raul...'

'Ally, please!' His eyes were pleading with her. His hand fastened round her wrist, his knuckles brushing the underside of her breast as he reached for her. 'Talk to me,' he said huskily. 'Put me out of my misery. Tell me you're not still in love with that bastard back in England?'

'Ally!'

The voice was amazingly familiar, considering she hadn't heard it for so long, but no less unwelcome because of that. Glancing round, she saw her ex-husband advancing across the lobby and her heart sank. In a short-sleeved cotton shirt and twill trousers, his jacket looped nonchalantly over one shoulder, Ally guessed Jeff considered he looked suave and stylish, but to her eyes he represented everything she'd learned to despise.

'Surprise, surprise,' he said, his tone not quite so confident now as he took in Ally's closeness to the man at her side. 'I guess you never expected to see me.'

Ally swallowed, casting an anxious look into Raul's frowning face. He didn't know who Jeff was yet, but he suspected it, and, after what he had just asked her, it was doubly distressing to see his hardening expression.

'I—as a matter of fact, I did,' Ally got out jerkily as Raul's hand fell away from her arm. 'Sam phoned me. She'd guessed where you'd gone.'

Jeff grimaced. 'She would,' he said irritably. Then, with another speculative glance at Raul, 'Aren't you going to say you're glad to see me, at least?' He hesitated for a moment, as if gauging what her relationship to the other man might be. But then, as if deciding that there could be nothing between them, he continued, 'I came all this way to see you.'

Raul stiffened. Although they weren't touching one another, Ally sensed his increasing withdrawal and her heart bled. Sensed, too, his increasing antipathy towards Jeff, and she wished with all her soul that she could reassure him. She wanted to tell him that she hadn't invited Jeff out here; that, in fact, she'd have done anything to avoid it happening. But she didn't have that right. Despite what he said, she had no rights where Raul was concerned. Anything there might have been between them would always be defeated by her age and his responsibilities...

# CHAPTER FOURTEEN

BUT nothing was stopping her from telling Jeff how she felt about this unwarranted intrusion into her holiday, Ally realised suddenly. She owed him no consideration. When had he ever considered her feelings? When had he ever cared about anyone but himself?

'I'm sorry but I'm not glad to see you, Jeff,' she said clearly, stepping back when he would have bent to kiss her cheek. The action brought her up against Raul's unyielding body and she was sorry about that, but when she tried to move away again, his hand on her hip kept her where she was. 'I—I didn't ask you to come here,' she continued, feeling the colour deepen in her throat. The heat of Raul's fingers was penetrating the thin layers of cloth and she was intensely aware of it. 'In—in fact,' she added unsteadily, 'I don't know why you've come.'

Jeff's blue eyes hardened and she wondered why she'd never noticed how closely set they were before. 'You know exactly why I'm here,' he insisted. 'God, if Sam warned you I was coming, she must have told you how disappointed I was when I got back and you weren't there.'

'Waiting for you, you mean?' asked Ally tightly, as Raul's hand tightened on her hip, his fingers slipping between the cropped top and her shorts, warm against her skin. 'It doesn't matter what Sam told me, Jeff. What you do has nothing to do with me any longer. We're divorced, in case you've forgotten. You made your life and I've made mine.'

'With him?' Jeff sneered, his eyes moving past his wife to fasten contemptuously on the man standing just behind her. 'Come off it, Ally. Who is he? One of the waiters?

150

Someone who's latched onto a lonely woman in the hope of getting something out of it, I bet.'

'You will take that back.'

Before Ally could react, she was moved unceremoniously aside, and Raul himself stepped forward. His anger fairly emanated from every pore and although Jeff must have been taken aback, his face took on a belligerent scowl.

'Who says?'

'I say,' said Raul, stepping nearer, his superior height and lean athletic build more than a match for the other man's much broader physique. 'Do you want to make something of it?'

'Oh, please…' Ally couldn't let this degenerate into a fight without at least trying to do something to stop it. 'There's no need for this.'

'There's every need,' Raul contradicted her chillingly, his dark eyes sparkling with a cold brilliance. 'This—person—insulted you and myself.'

Jeff hunched his shoulders. 'You're very touchy for someone who makes his living preying on innocent women,' he muttered barely audibly, but Raul heard him and the next second he had a handful of Jeff's expensive sports shirt in his fist.

'What did you say?' he demanded, and at last Jeff seemed to realise that Raul meant what he said.

'Hey,' he protested weakly, tugging at Raul's wrist. 'D'you know how much this shirt cost me?'

'Much more than you're worth, I'm sure,' responded Raul, tightening his hold, and Jeff winced.

'You're hurting me,' he cried, his eyes turning to his ex-wife in desperate appeal. 'For pity's sake, Ally, I didn't mean any harm. Get him off me!'

'Raul—'

'I haven't heard your apology yet,' Raul declared, ignoring her, his attention totally focussed on the other man. Jeff had dropped his jacket now and was using both hands to try and free himself, but without any success. Raul seemed invincible and if Ally hadn't been so involved, she'd have found the whole affair laughable.

As, indeed, did many of the hotel's guests who were gradually gathering to watch them. There was a buzz of interested speculation and Ally realised something had to be done. All it needed was for Suzanne or Julia or even Peter to come into the lobby to see what was going on and God knew what might happen.

'Raul,' she said again, her voice low but audible. Her fist balled at the thought of touching him, but she forced her fingers to uncurl and brush anxiously at his arm. 'Please, Raul, let him go.'

Raul turned his head to look at her. 'You do not mind that this man insulted you?' he asked icily, and Ally shook her head, as much in an effort to clear it as in answer to his question. But Raul didn't know that.

'I—'

'That's what the lady's saying, man.' Before she could explain what she really meant, Jeff broke in, his smug tone an indication that he thought he'd won. 'Hey, Ally and I have been married for a considerable number of years. We understand one another, don't we, sweetheart? Come on: let me go—Raul, is it? Yeah, yeah.' This as Raul shoved him away. 'That's better. That's much better.'

As Jeff bent to pick up his jacket, Ally looked at Raul and she wanted to die at the expression on his face. It encompassed so much: pain; bewilderment; *contempt*. But most of all betrayal, and Ally guessed that by taking Jeff's side she had destroyed whatever it was that had been between them.

The other guests were all drifting away now, probably disappointed that it hadn't developed into a full-scale fight. But Ally could only be relieved on that score. She wished she could drift away, too. She wanted nothing so much as to be alone to nurse her wounded spirit, but she was compelled to stay and ensure that nothing worse happened.

'Ally...' Just when she'd been sure that Raul would never want to speak to her again, he touched her arm. 'We haven't finished our conversation.' He cast a sideways look at Jeff. 'Can I ring you later?'

Ally didn't know what to say. She was intensely aware of Jeff watching them and listening to every word, and, while he was silent at the moment, she knew him well enough to know that if he was pushed into a corner, he'd show no compunction about hurting her in any way he could. And once he found out who Raul really was, who he was going to marry...

'I think you'd better go, Raul,' she said stiffly, hating to have to disillusion him again, and, as if he had only been waiting for some sign that Ally still cared about him, Jeff added his voice to hers.

'You heard the lady,' he said, brave now that the danger was past, and Ally wanted to put her fist into his conceited face.

'I'm sorry, Raul,' she muttered, but Raul was already turning away, and she watched helplessly as he strode across the lobby and out through the glass doors.

'Good riddance,' said Jeff, staring after him. 'You're well rid of him, Ally. I knew what he was about the minute I saw him.'

'You don't know anything, Jeff,' retorted Ally harshly, avoiding the attempt he made to take her arm. 'As far as I'm concerned, you can go, too. If I never see you again, it'll be too soon.'

'You don't mean that, Ally?'

He stared at her, aghast, but Ally had had quite enough for one day. 'Don't I?' she asked scornfully. 'Well, if you hang around long enough, you'll find out.' She moved away from him. 'And now, I want to have a word with Suzanne.'

Jeff stared at her. 'Surely you're going to give me a chance to explain why I'm here,' he protested.

'I know why you're here, Jeff,' she told him coldly. 'Living with Kelly hasn't worked out so you went back to England hoping I'd be willing to let you weep on my shoulder. Well, you were wrong.'

Jeff gasped. 'You sound so hard, Ally.'

'Just practical,' she said, realising she had been a fool to be afraid of seeing him again. If ever she'd had any feelings for Jeff, they were long gone. All she felt now was a sense of regret for all the years she'd wasted.

'But you love me, Ally!'

Jeff wasn't prepared to accept what she'd said and Ally raised her eyes heavenward. If she wasn't careful, this was going to run into another noisy confrontation and she couldn't have that. Heaving a sigh, she gestured towards the public lounge that opened off the lobby. 'Let's go in there,' she said, guessing correctly that it would be deserted at this time of the afternoon. 'We can't hear ourselves speak here.'

Which wasn't precisely true, but Jeff seemed to agree with her, and, as she had expected, the pleasant palm-fringed sitting room was empty. Most guests were sunning themselves by the pool or taking a rest before Happy Hour. Ally wished that was all she had on her mind. She'd never dreamt her holiday would prove as eventful as it had.

'You love me, Ally,' Jeff said again, when they were facing one another in the sun-dappled parlour. 'You know you do. There's no point in trying to pretend you don't.'

Ally was stunned at his conceit. 'You're wrong, Jeff,' she stated flatly. 'I once thought I loved you, but I know better now. I'm sorry you've had a wasted journey. I had no idea you might come out here until Sam found you'd gone.'

'Is it because of him?' Jeff flicked a thumb towards the lobby and Ally's heart flipped a beat at the thought of the damage he could do.

'I—no, of course not,' she replied hurriedly. 'R—Raul is just a friend, that's all.'

'Come off it, Ally.' Jeff was scornful now. 'I know a come-on when I see it. The guy was fairly eating you with his eyes.' He snorted. 'He must be a sucker for older women, eh?'

'You're wrong—'

'I don't think so.' Somehow Jeff had detected that there was more to this than she was saying. And, because he was feeling aggrieved over the way she'd treated him, he was looking for any little thing to taunt her with. 'Way to go, Ally. It's not every day you get to have sex with a stud like him. However doubtful his motives might be.'

'Jeff, for God's sake!'

Ally was horrified, but the more agitated she became, the more she convinced him that he'd hit a nerve. 'Hey, who am I to talk?' he drawled, looping his jacket over his shoulder again and smirking at her. 'Kelly wasn't exactly middle-aged; I know that. And believe me, I can understand the attraction of firm young flesh—'

'You're disgusting!' Ally was sickened by his attitude. And the knowledge that he could say all these things to Suzanne as well was doubly disturbing. Dear God, she couldn't let him talk to the Davises. If he even so much as hinted at a relationship between her and Raul...

And, as if he could read her thoughts, Jeff braced a hand on his hip and said softly, 'But I'm right, aren't I? You and the stud—you have been to bed together. Don't bother to deny it. I can see it in your eyes. You always were too transparent for your own good.'

Ally shook her head. 'You're mistaken...'

'Am I?' Jeff arched a sardonic brow. 'Perhaps I should ask Suzanne. I'm sure she'll be only too eager to put me right on that score. Seeing as how she's always hated my guts.'

Ally's breath escaped on a little gasp. 'Y—you can't ask Suzanne.'

'Why can't I?' Once again she had betrayed her hand, and Ally wanted to scream at her own stupidity. 'Doesn't she know about your little liaison?'

Ally was desperate. 'It's nothing to do with Suzanne.'

'So you haven't told her.' Jeff's lips pursed. 'Interesting.' He frowned. 'God, he's not her son, is he?' He uttered a short laugh. 'If he is, I can understand why you might have reservations about discussing it with her.'

'He's not her son.' Ally's face was burning. 'Suzanne doesn't have a son; only a daughter.'

'Is that right?' Jeff regarded her thoughtfully. 'Pity.'

'You are—contemptible,' said Ally chokingly. 'You judge everyone by your own—repulsive standards.'

'Maybe so.' Jeff wasn't offended. 'But you have to admit I'm on the right track. There's something about this affair— if you'll pardon the pun—that doesn't ring true.'

'You're exaggerating, as usual.'

'Am I?' Again, Jeff wasn't convinced. 'Why does the idea of me telling Suzanne about your admirer upset you so? It can't just be because you're ashamed of taking a lover. Dammit all, in your position, I'd probably have done the same.'

Ally grimaced. 'Is that supposed to be some sort of endorsement?'

'No.' Jeff's frown deepened. 'But I wouldn't be so quick to cast judgement, if I were you. You know what they say about people in glass houses. And I have to tell you, in your position I'd be a little chary about throwing stones.'

'What do you mean?'

'I mean, I make a better friend than I do an enemy.'

Ally gasped. 'Are you threatening me?'

Jeff shrugged. 'Whatever it takes.'

'Why are you doing this?'

'Why do you think?' Jeff reached out and caught her chin

in his hand. 'Like you said before, I want you back. And if, to achieve that, I have to use a little gentle—blackmail—well, that's the way it goes.'

'You're despicable.' Ally dragged herself away from him.

'So you keep saying. Keep it up and I may just decide that Suzanne deserves to know what you've been doing in her hotel.' His lips twisted. 'It's up to you.' He glanced about him. 'Personally I'm not averse to spending a few days in this island paradise. According to the travel agent in Newcastle, the Davises have plenty of guest rooms vacant.'

Ally stared at him. 'You can't stay here.'

'Why not?'

'I—Suzanne would never let you.'

'I don't think even Suzanne would want to run foul of the tourist board. I mean, she has no reason to refuse to accommodate me. I don't drink too much. I don't even smoke. And as far as bothering the other guests are concerned...'

Ally held up her head. 'I don't want you here, Jeff.'

'Hell, I know that.' He chuckled. 'Tough luck.'

'You don't understand.' Ally took a deep breath. 'I had planned on leaving today.'

'Leaving?' Jeff's brows drew together. 'To go where?'

'Where do you think?'

'Back to England?'

Ally nodded.

Jeff shook his head. 'I don't believe you.'

'You should. It's true.' Crossing her fingers in the pockets of her shorts, Ally looked at him. 'Sam was—worried about you.' She prayed her daughter would forgive her. 'I told her I was coming back today.'

# CHAPTER FIFTEEN

'THERE'S a phone call for you, Mrs Sloan.'

Ally looked up from the spreadsheet she'd been studying to find a glamorous young woman leaning over her desk. Jennifer Morrell was the boss's secretary here at Jedburgh Transport and it was obvious from her expression that she resented having to deliver a message to one of the lowlier members of the staff.

'A phone call?' Ally felt a wedge of apprehension rise to lodge itself in her throat. 'Who—who is it?'

'Your daughter, I think,' said Jennifer shortly, and Ally breathed a little easier. 'I didn't ask. You know Mr Jedburgh doesn't like anyone taking private calls during office hours.'

'I know.'

Ally's response was apologetic, but inside she was a seething mass of doubts and frustrations. She'd been like this ever since she got back from San Cristobál, and even the fact that Jeff seemed to have accepted that he was wasting his time and she wasn't going to take him back hadn't helped. She was far too conscious of the power he had over her and, although there was a good four thousand miles between San Cristobál and here, she still wasn't convinced he wouldn't take it into his head to tell Suzanne what had been going on.

Of course, there was always the chance that Suzanne would refuse to speak to him. Her friend hadn't taken Ally's decision to return to England with her ex-husband at all well, and she'd blamed Jeff for ruining Ally's holiday.

Which wasn't altogether fair, Ally acknowledged ruefully. She had ruined it herself long before she'd got to the island. She just hadn't known it at the time.

158

In any event, returning to England had been her only option then. Somehow, she had had to get Jeff out of the hotel before either Suzanne or Peter saw him and precipitated the kind of scene she'd dreaded most. If he had been challenged Jeff would have had no compunction about telling Suzanne what her precious friend had been up to—though even he could have had no idea how destructive that would be.

Consequently, Ally had had to persuade him that it was in his best interests to return to the airport at San Cristobál and wait for her there. There'd been a flight back to London at ten o'clock that night and, as she'd had Mike Mclean's number, it had been a simple matter to phone him and arrange for him to fly them to Nassau in the early evening.

At the time, Jeff had demurred, of course. He'd just arrived, and Ally guessed he'd been hoping to plead his case in San Cristobál's semi-tropical surroundings. But somehow she'd managed to convince him that unless he agreed to her terms, she'd return to England without him and that would defeat his objective anyway. And, because he still hadn't been able to believe that ultimately she would turn him down, he'd agreed.

The interview she'd had with Suzanne had not been pleasant. Her friend had been in a bad mood to begin with and she hadn't been able to see any reason whatsoever why Ally should feel any obligation towards her ex-husband. And because she hadn't known that Jeff was on the island, she'd considered Ally's sudden departure to be both foolish and ungrateful.

And it had been, thought Ally now, abruptly becoming aware that Jennifer was still standing by her desk staring at her with wide impatient eyes. She was obviously waiting for Ally to answer the phone which was situated on her desk, and her toe was tapping a frustrated tattoo on the rubber-tiled floor.

Pushing up from her desk, Ally hoped it was Sam on the other end of the line. Ever since her return, she'd been dreading a call from Suzanne, demanding to know why she hadn't mentioned the fact that Jeff had been responsible for her precipitate decision to return to England. Mike was bound to have told her friend that she'd had company on the flight, particularly as her companion had had the same surname as herself. She still hadn't thought of a convincing reason why she'd kept Jeff's arrival to herself, and she was hoping that, if Suzanne did find out, she'd assume Ally hadn't told her because she'd known how angry Suzanne would be.

Angry! Ally shivered. Thank God Suzanne hadn't had a chance to confront Jeff with her opinion of him. In those circumstances, there would have been only one outcome, and Ally would have been the loser on all counts.

Trying not to be aware of Jennifer, who had now resumed her seat at her desk, Ally picked up the receiver. 'Hello,' she said nervously, pressing a hand to her stomach. 'Is that you, Sam?'

'Yeah, Mum. It's me.' Ally's relief was tempered by the unfamiliar excitement in her daughter's voice. 'How are you?'

'How am I—?' Ally realised she was repeating her daughter's words and, conscious of Jennifer's sullen attention, she took a steadying breath. 'I only saw you at breakfast, Sam. You know how I am.'

'Are you sitting down?'

'Am I—?' Once again, Ally was compelled to press her lips together to silence the impatient words. 'No, I'm not,' she said shortly. And then, as another, less appealing, thought occurred to her, she said, 'What's happened? Has there been an accident or something?'

'How your mind does leap to the worst-case scenario,' exclaimed Sam drily. 'No, there hasn't been an accident. Not as far as I know anyway. Dad called earlier this morning, but it was just to tell me that he's going for an interview for a job in North Shields, and I doubt Ryan is even out of bed

yet. It is only twelve o'clock, you know,' she added sardon-
ically.

'Then why—?'

'If you'll stop jumping to conclusions, I'll tell you,' replied Sam mildly, and, unable to stand Jennifer's appraisal
any longer, Ally turned her back on her.

'I wish you would,' she said in a low impatient voice.
'I've got work to do.'

'Oh, well, if you feel like that—'

'Sam!'

Ally spoke through her teeth and, as if taking pity on her,
Sam gave in. 'You've had a visitor,' she said without further
preamble. 'Does the name Rafael Ramirez mean anything to
you?'

'Raf—*Raul!*' Ally's legs simply refused to support her
and, uncaring at that moment what Jennifer might think, she
hooked a trembling hip over a corner of the desk. She licked
her dry lips. 'Raul—is—is there?'

'He was,' agreed Sam, apparently pleased at her parent's
reaction to her news. 'He's quite a hunk, isn't he?'

Ally didn't know how to answer her. 'Wh—what did he
want?' she asked, while her mind posed and rejected all the
reasons why Raul might be in the north-east of England.
Although there were boatyards in the area producing the
kind of craft his father chartered to holidaymakers, companies, and the like, she couldn't believe he had come so far
to place an order he could have made at the Boat Show over
a month ago.

'Don't you know?' asked Sam, turning the question back
on her, and, realising she couldn't go on conducting this
conversation in the presence of an audience, Ally made a
decision.

'I'm coming home,' she said, uncaring that Jennifer
sucked in an indignant breath behind her. 'I'll be with you
in fifteen minutes.'

As luck would have it, Andy Jedburgh was out of the

office that morning. Ignoring Jennifer's shrill warning that
he wouldn't like her leaving without finishing the salary
spreadsheets, Ally forced her unsteady legs to carry her
across the car park to where she'd left her second-hand Mini.
It only took her a few minutes to reach the small house in
Penrose Terrace that she shared with her daughter, and Sam
opened the door as she walked up the path.

'Hey,' she exclaimed, as Ally pushed past her into the
house. 'I'm sorry if I gave you a shock.' She viewed her
mother's retreating back with some concern. 'I thought
you'd want to know that he was here.'

Ally shook her head, going straight down the narrow hall
to the small kitchen, filling the kettle and plugging it in
before answering her. Then, when she was sure she could
face Sam without betraying how she really felt, she turned
and said tightly, 'What did he want? Did he say why he'd
come?' And then, less surely, 'Is he coming back?'

Sam looked anxious. 'I think you ought to sit down and
have a cup of tea first, Mum,' she said, trying to be helpful.
'You look so pale.'

'I'm all right.'

'You're not all right.' Sam sighed. 'Do you want to tell
me what's going on?'

'I don't know what's—' Ally started to make some excuse, but, if he was really here, her daughter deserved at
least part of the truth. 'Honestly, Sam, I never thought I'd
ever see Raul again.'

'Raul?' Sam looked puzzled for a moment. Then her face
cleared. 'Oh, right. That's what you call him, is it?'

'It's what everybody calls him, except his parents,' said
Ally steadily and Sam's eyes went wide.

'Oh, wow! You've met his parents!'

'Well, yes.' Ally was afraid her daughter was getting totally the wrong impression. 'But it's not what you think. I
only met them because they're friends of Suzanne and
Peter.'

'So did Aunt Suzanne introduce you?'

'No.' Ally drew her lower lip between her teeth, trying to think of an appropriate response. 'I—we—met at the hotel in London. Before I flew out.'

'I see.' Sam digested this. 'So is he the man you've been seeing while you were away?' Her expression was incredulous. 'God, Mum, no wonder you were so cagey about him!'

'Why?' Ally stared at her daughter. 'Because he's so much younger than me?' she demanded, and Sam's cheeks turned a little pink.

'No—'

'You don't need to lie, Sam.'

'I'm not lying.' Sam drew a breath. 'Honestly, Mum. His age has nothing to do with it. What is he? A couple of years younger than you? That's nothing nowadays.'

'Then—'

'Oh, come on, Mum.' Sam was uncomfortable. 'I mean, you are attractive. And that tan you acquired in San Cristobál really brings out the green in your eyes. Even the streaks in your hair—well, you should have had them done years ago. But—but—'

'I'm not the kind of woman to attract a man like Raul Ramirez? Is that what you're saying?'

'Sort of.' Sam's face was red. 'Help me out here, Mum. Are you saying he really is interested in you?'

'I don't know.' Even now, Ally couldn't admit it. Turning away, she busied herself by setting out two cups and taking a carton of milk from the fridge. 'What did he say?'

'What did he say?' Sam repeated the words, clearly trying to remember. 'Well, he wanted to see you, obviously. He asked where you were and I told him you were at work.'

'Just like that?' Ally glanced over her shoulder. 'A strange man comes to the door and asks you where I am and you tell him?'

'No. Not like that,' exclaimed Sam defensively. 'He knew

who I was. When I opened the door, he said "You must be Sam", or something like that, and he disarmed me.'

'He does that.' Ally bent her head over the teabags. 'Then what?'

'Oh—' Sam tried to think. 'He asked if I would tell you he was here, in England, and that you—you could reach him at the Post House if you wanted to speak to him.'

'The Post House?' Ally swung round. 'Is that what he said?'

'Yes.' Sam moistened her lips. 'Are—are you going to see him?'

Ally expelled a breath. 'I don't know.'

Sam gasped. 'What's not to know? Either you are or you aren't?' Her brows drew together. 'Hey, does Dad know about him?'

'Why do you ask?'

'Just something he said.'

Ally felt a twinge of apprehension. 'What? What did he say?'

'Oh, Mum.' Sam shook her head. 'I can't remember everything everybody says.' She considered. 'I don't know. I didn't take much notice of it at the time. I just thought he was being grumpy because you'd refused to take him back.'

'How grumpy?'

Sam sighed. 'Well, he said something about you making a fool of him. That he shouldn't have believed you when you insisted that you weren't involved with anyone else.'

Ally's lips parted in dismay. 'So why didn't you tell me?'

'Oh, right.' Sam was sardonic. 'What was there to tell, Mum? He didn't mention any names. He just said he wished he'd told Aunt Suzanne what a liar you are. I was hardly likely to tell you that. As a matter of fact, I warned him not to make those kind of allegations about you. As far as I knew you weren't seriously seeing anyone else.'

'And I'm not,' said Ally swiftly. 'Oh, Sam, you don't think he could have phoned Suzanne, do you?'

'What if he did?' Sam was confused. 'Why would it matter? Aunt Suzanne has nothing to do with this.'

'She does!' Ally was distraught. 'Oh, Sam, Raul is Julia's boyfriend. Suzanne and Peter are expecting them to get engaged soon.'

Sam's jaw dropped. 'You're kidding!'

'No, I'm not.'

'But he must be years older than Julia.'

'Not that much,' said Ally flatly. 'It's less than the difference there is between Raul and me. He's only twenty-nine, Sam. I'm nearly ten years older than he is.'

Sam studied her mother's face. 'And that matters to you?'

'Doesn't it matter to you?' countered Ally, and Sam lifted her arms to clasp the back of her neck with both hands.

'Me?' she echoed. 'Why should it bother me?' She blinked. 'Are you saying there is something between you?'

Ally shook her head. 'I don't know what to think any more.'

Sam tried to understand what her mother was saying. 'Let me get this straight,' she said carefully. 'How does Dad know about it—if indeed he does?'

'Oh—he saw us together,' answered Ally wearily. 'I was on my way to tell Suzanne that I was leaving when Raul intercepted me in the—in the lobby.'

'And what?' Sam's eyes were wide. 'Was Raul kissing you or—'

'Nothing like that,' exclaimed Ally, her own face burning now. 'We were just—talking, that's all.'

Sam's arms dropped to her sides. 'And Dad could tell from that that you and this Raul were having an affair?' She made a disbelieving gesture. 'I don't think so.'

'All right.' With some misgivings, Ally gave her daughter a brief description of the events that had precipitated Raul's attack on Jeff. 'So now you see it isn't as unlikely as it sounds.'

'Hey.' Sam couldn't prevent an illicit giggle. 'And I

thought you led such a boring life. I bet Daddy didn't like that.'

'He didn't.' Ally nodded her agreement. 'That was when I knew I had to get him out of the hotel. If he'd told Suzanne…'

'Do you think he has?' asked Sam suddenly. 'Do you think that's why this Raul has come here? Because his relationship with Julia is off?'

Ally didn't want to believe it, but it had the ring of truth about it. 'I hope not,' she said, squashing the germ of hope that had seeded in her belly when she'd thought Raul had been prepared to tell Julia the truth rather than let her go. But that was foolish, she conceded unhappily. It had been three weeks since she'd left the island. Much too long for Raul to make up his own mind.

'What do you mean, you hope not?' Sam asked now. 'Correct me if I'm wrong, but I've been getting the distinct impression that you—that you care about this man. Don't you care if he marries someone else?'

'It's nothing to do with me.' Ally refused to discuss the Davises' problems with her daughter.

'You wish.' Sam stared at her. 'Are you peeved because you think Dad may have spilled the beans to Aunt Suzanne?'

It was easier to let Sam think that. 'Perhaps,' said Ally, amazed that her hand was steady enough to make the tea. She set the cups and milk on a tray to carry into the living room. 'I'd better have this and then get back to work.'

'But—' Sam was incredulous. 'Aren't you going to ring— Raul?'

'I don't think so,' said Ally carefully, lifting the tray and brushing past her daughter. 'Don't look at me like that, Sam. I know what I'm doing. As you said before, men like Raul Ramirez don't get seriously involved with women like me.'

# CHAPTER SIXTEEN

WHICH was all well and good, but Ally found it incredibly hard to justify her decision to herself during the long afternoon that followed. Whatever had brought Raul to England—and she couldn't believe he'd travelled all this way just to see her—it would still have been good to see him again.

So good, she mused wistfully, grateful when the clock on the office wall crawled round to five o'clock and she could leave. Coming back to England, having to deal with Jeff's thwarted ambitions, even returning to work and the day-to-day routine she was used to, had helped to assuage the anguish she'd felt when she'd left San Cristobál, but it hadn't lasted. As each succeeding week went by, it got harder and harder to sleep at night. Images of herself and Raul together, their naked bodies hot and sweaty from the heat of their lovemaking, dampened her body and quickened her pulse. Some nights they totally refused to be dislodged and the memory of how he'd looked when she'd sent him away was a constant torment.

Of course, she'd believed that she'd never have the chance to see him again. She'd assumed that, whatever they'd shared, he would eventually marry Julia and produce the grandchildren his parents craved. She guessed he'd think that she and Jeff would get back together again, too. That, however much she'd denied it, the fact that she'd taken her ex-husband's part over his, was proof that she hadn't meant what she said.

But now all her preconceived ideas of the future had been thrown into confusion. She didn't know what was happening any more and, despite what she'd said to Sam, the temptation to see him just one more time was almost irresistible.

There was a note from her daughter waiting for her when she got home. Ally was aware that her hands were trembling as she picked it up, but it wasn't about Raul. Sam merely said that she'd be working until seven o'clock and then she was going to her fiancé's home for supper. She didn't know what time she'd be back, she'd added, but Ally shouldn't wait up. Mark would see she got home safely whatever time it was.

Ally gave a rueful sigh. Lucky Sam, she thought wryly. Her daughter was so sure about her future. There'd be no unplanned pregnancies for her; no marriage based on need rather than love.

She dropped the note again and turned away. So she had the evening to herself. She was disappointed, really. She had hoped Sam would come home after she finished at the restaurant. She'd wanted to talk to her; to ask her more about Raul, if she was honest. But Sam evidently thought her mother had said all she was going to say and had decided to leave the subject of her relationship with Raul alone.

Tactful, Ally supposed gloomily. She had been rather impatient about it at lunchtime and she had only herself to blame if her daughter had taken her at her word.

Compellingly, the thought of Raul, dining alone at the Post House Hotel, popped into her head. She wondered what he was doing at this moment, whether he'd taken the chance to explore the city or was sitting in his room, waiting for her to call.

He'd wait a long time, she told herself fiercely. How could she call him? How could she expect her to pick up the phone and speak to him as if his turning up here in Newcastle was a perfectly natural thing for him to do? She wasn't like him; he knew that. Therefore he should know that she was too practical—too *old*—to play fast and loose with other people's lives.

*Yet he was here...*

She forced that thought back into the recesses of her mind, trying to tell herself that she mustn't fall into the trap of believing he had come all this way just to see her. He wouldn't have. He *couldn't* have.

*So why was he here?*

Ally dropped her coat over the back of a chair and made her way upstairs. She was not going to think about it any more, she decided. All she was doing was tearing away the small veneer of normality she'd achieved during the past three weeks. All right, she didn't sleep well and she suffered a lot of stress, but eventually—eventually—she would be able to put all this behind her. She had to. *She had to.*

She paused in front of the mirror in her bedroom. God, she looked a mess, she thought. The highlights in her hair were beginning to fade, and if she wasn't careful she'd begin to see herself as she was before she went to San Cristóbal. Even her face was pale, and the flattering suntan she had acquired on the island had lost its glow.

Shaking her head, she turned away, and as she did so, an idea occurred to her: perhaps she ought to agree to see Raul, after all. Here, without the deceptive trappings of sophistication her holiday had given her, he would see her as she really was. Not the sun-tanned temptress he'd pretended she represented, but a harassed housewife, with little claim to either sophistication or beauty.

She swallowed the sudden constriction she felt in her throat. The idea of ringing Raul and arranging to meet him at some neutral location was terrifying. Despite what she kept telling herself, she was very much afraid that if she did see him again, she wouldn't be able to hide how she felt about him. And it would be too humiliating if she gave herself away...

She couldn't do it. Knowing herself for a coward, Ally went into the bathroom and turned on the taps. Then, going downstairs again, she rescued the solitary bottle of German

white from the fridge, opening it and collecting a glass before going back upstairs again.

She wished she could get drunk, she thought miserably,
stripping off her clothes before stepping into the tub. That
way she might be able to silence the clamouring voices in
her head that warned her this might be her last chance for
happiness.

She was on her third glass of wine when the doorbell rang.

Determining to ignore it, Ally nestled down into the
foamy water, only to feel a twinge of anxiety when the bell
rang for a second time. Damn, she thought uneasily. Had
she left her key in the lock? She remembered locking the
door as she came in, but she didn't remember taking the key
out of the lock again. Both Sam and Ryan had keys, of
course, but they couldn't use them if her key was still in the
lock.

She hesitated only a moment longer before putting down
her glass and getting out of the bath. Then, wrapping a towel
sarongwise beneath her arms, she opened the bathroom door
and went to the top of the stairs. From there, she could see
the front door with her key sticking plainly out of the lock.
But, by the light of the street lamp outside, she could also
see the unmistakable silhouette of a man, and her pulse began to race.

It was Raul. She knew it. The silhouette was much too
tall for either Ryan or Sam's fiancé, and even as she stood
there, frozen to the spot, he rattled the letterbox and called,
'Ally! I know you're in there. Your car's parked outside.'

Ally blinked, wondering how he had known that it was
her car. He didn't know what kind of car she drove.
Unless…unless Sam had told him…

The possible implications of the note her daughter had
left her were suddenly clear. She had been wrong to think
that Sam had accepted her decision. Her daughter, who knew
her almost as well as she knew herself, had immediately

done what she herself had been afraid to do: she had rung Raul.

Realising she couldn't pretend any longer, Ally called, 'I'll be right down,' and scurried back into the bathroom.

Another glance at her reflection was no more reassuring than it had been before. She'd washed her hair, but, although it was clean, it was still wet. Shedding the bath-towel, she replaced it with her woollen dressing gown and, going into the bedroom, she skewered her hair on top of her head with a tortoiseshell clip. Then, without giving herself time to have second thoughts, she pushed her feet into heelless mules and went quickly down the stairs.

A draught of cold air enveloped her as she opened the door, and she shivered. But she knew the feathering of her spine owed more to the man who was waiting on her doorstep, one hand raised to support himself against the wall, than to the chilling wind. She'd never seen him in an overcoat before, the grey cashmere parting to reveal black moleskin trousers and a turtle-necked grey sweater.

'Raul,' she said artlessly, as if she hadn't known it was him until she opened the door. 'Um—you'd better come in.'

'Thank you.'

He straightened, and stepped over the threshold, and Ally moved aside to let him advance into the hall. The narrow passageway was immediately dwarfed by his presence, and, suppressing the gulp that threatened to betray her, she closed the door again and said, 'Please: go into the living room. I won't be a minute. I'll just go and put some clothes on—'

'No.' Although she'd thought he was going to do as she'd asked, he turned in the doorway to the living room and confronted her. It was the first opportunity she'd had to see him clearly and she was disturbed to see that he looked thinner, his face pale and weary. 'No, don't go and put your clothes on,' he said heavily. 'Please. I like you just the way you are.'

Ally stared at him. 'I—' She didn't know how to deal
with this. 'Why have you come here, Raul?'

Raul gave her an old-fashioned look. 'Like you don't
know.'

'I don't know.' Ally wrapped her arms about her midriff.
'Are you on your own?'

'Who would I be with?' Raul closed his eyes for a moment and then opened them again on a drawn-out sigh.
'Okay,' he said, reaching out a hand and gripping her two
arms where they crossed at her waist. 'Come in here and I'll
tell you.'

Ally quivered. She couldn't help it. Just being near to him,
having him touch her—albeit through the sleeves of her old
dressing gown—was overpowering and she couldn't hide
her reaction from him.

'Oh, Ally,' he muttered, feeling her trembling, and, aban-
doning for the moment any attempt to explain his actions,
he pulled her against him. 'Ally, you have no idea of the
torment you've put me through.'

Ally rather thought she had, but for the moment she was
wantonly content to feel his mouth moving on hers, rubbing
sensuously against her lips, tasting her and provoking her,
until she reached up with both hands and fastened her mouth
to his.

She'd thought she'd remembered everything about him,
but she hadn't. She'd forgotten how devastating his lovemaking could be and she heard him stifle a groan as he
gathered her closer into his arms.

She realised that he was trembling, too, his lean muscular
body shuddering as he parted his legs to bring her nearer.
Although she tried to remember that there had always been
this sexual attraction between them, that she shouldn't mistake lust for love, for now it was enough that he was holding
her and caressing her, his voice hoarse and muffled when he
released her mouth to burrow his face into her neck.

'Dear God, Ally,' he muttered, his breath hot against her

ear, 'why did you let me go on thinking that you and Jeff were going home to try and make another attempt at your marriage? I've gone through hell thinking that you and that smug bastard were back together again.'

Ally caught her breath as his hand invaded the neckline of her gown and his thumb found the swollen peak of her breast. For a moment, she couldn't trust herself to speak, and, taking advantage of the fact, Raul drew his hand down and parted the loose cord that kept the two sides of the dressing gown in place.

'You—you know why I did it,' Ally got out at last, trying to cover herself again—without a great deal of success. 'You were going to marry Julia and—'

'But I'd already told Suzanne that I wasn't going to marry Julia,' said Raul thickly, his eyes dropping possessively to the triangle of honey-coloured hair at the apex of her thighs. Then, forcing his head up again, he rested his forehead against hers as he added, 'Dammit, that was why I had had that meeting with the Davises that day—Jeff—turned up at the hotel.'

Ally's groan was anguished. 'Oh, Raul, you didn't!'

'Yes, I did,' he told her roughly, his eyes darkening with sudden impatience. 'Why? Why should it matter to you? Did you want me to marry Julia? Is that it? Did you prefer the freedom of an illicit affair to the responsibilities of a real relationship?'

Ally's mouth dropped. 'How can you ask me that?' she asked in horror. Dragging herself away from him, she wrapped her gown about her again. 'How can you ask me *that*?'

'Hey, I'm going to be asking you a hell of a lot more than that,' he declared harshly, flinging off his coat and turning away to push agitated fingers through his hair. 'Like who do you think is the injured party here? Like how could you leave knowing how much I cared about you?'

Ally shook her head. 'You know how it was,' she protested. 'I thought you were going to marry Julia...'

'But Suzanne must have told you that was off,' he argued, turning on the hearth to look across the room at her. He scowled. 'I was sure she would.'

'Well, she didn't,' said Ally tremulously. 'I'm not a liar.'

'And nor am I,' said Raul steadily. 'I love you, Ally. Are you going to tell me that's wrong?'

Ally's jaw quivered. 'But—but Suzanne was depending on you.'

Raul's brows drew together. 'For what?'

Ally lifted her shoulders in a helpless gesture. 'You must know,' she said pleadingly. 'Don't make me say it.'

'Ah.' Raul took a step in her direction. 'I assume you're talking about the loan.'

Ally nodded.

'Are you saying that Suzanne had confided her troubles to you and didn't tell you that they'd been settled?'

Ally's eyes widened. 'I don't understand.'

'Obviously not.' Raul came a little nearer. 'I was sure you would have been the first to know.'

'That your father was likely to call in the loan he'd offered them at the time he thought you and Julia were going to get married?' she exclaimed. 'I don't think so.'

'No.' Raul sighed. 'That my father had agreed to write off the loan in exchange for an agreed share in the hotel. It was what the Davises had suggested when they first approached my father for a loan, only at that time he preferred not to become involved in the business.'

'They approached your father?' Ally was stunned. That was not what Suzanne had told her. 'I had no idea.'

'No.' Raul came to stand in front of her. 'I believe you.' He trailed a seductive finger down her hot cheek. 'I'm sorry. I naturally assumed they'd have told you.'

Ally didn't know what to say, what to do. 'So—your father had a change of heart,' she whispered. 'Why?'

'Oh, I think he can see the writing on the wall,' replied Raul drily. 'Carlos is in love with Julia and, as the Davises have no son to carry on the business after they retire, I think my father is taking a stake in Carlos's future.'

Ally couldn't believe it. 'And you don't mind?'

'Mind?' Raul's finger explored the contours of her mouth. 'Why would I mind? I told you why I'd got involved with Julia that night at Finisterre. The night you told me in no uncertain terms that you weren't interested in me.'

'That's not true.' Ally balled one fist and pressed it into the palm of her other hand, gazing up at him with wide anxious eyes. 'You know—you know why I said what I did. I've explained that.' She made a helpless little gesture. 'I just don't know what—what you want of me?'

'Oh, I think you do.' Raul's voice had thickened, and his hand had slipped around her neck, warm against the damp hair that was gradually freeing itself from the clip. 'I want you.' He drew her towards him. 'And I think you want me, only you're too damned proud to say so.'

'It's not pride,' said Ally unsteadily, when he bent his head to nuzzle her ear, and Raul gave a rueful laugh.

'Well, whatever it is, I want you to say it,' he murmured, finding her mouth and biting the soft inner flesh. 'I want you to say, I want you, Raul. Just as much as you want me.'

'Oh, I do.' Ally's voice wobbled as she said the words. 'I want you, Raul. I want you to make love to me. I want to make love to you.' She gave a tremulous smile. 'Will that do?'

'For now,' agreed Raul against her lips, and she gave herself up to the eager passion of his kiss.

They were hungry for one another, and for a few moments there was no sound but the laboured urgency of their breathing. And Ally realised that, whatever he wanted, she had to have him in her life, even if it meant sharing him with some other woman who could give him the children he owed his mother.

Desperately, she drew him closer, her hands slipping beneath the hem of his sweater, to find the warm skin beneath. He was so smooth, so supple, and she dipped her hands into the waistband of his trousers, feeling a thrill of possession when he bucked against her exploring fingers.

'God, Ally' he groaned, dragging her hands around to the front of his trousers and pressing them against the hard ridge that swelled beneath the cloth. With infinite tenderness, she traced the throbbing length of his erection, but when her fingers searched for his zip, he uttered a protesting groan. 'Not yet,' he said, backing up against the sofa, and, with a rueful smile, he subsided onto the cushions, pulling her down on top of him.

Her robe was easily disposed of and then she took the greatest pleasure in helping him push his sweater over his head. She'd forgotten how broad his chest was, forgotten how tantalising the fine covering of coarse hair that arrowed down into his trousers.

Straddling him, she unbuckled his belt and opened his zip. He was wearing navy briefs tonight and he groaned again when she didn't immediately release him from their confinement but merely stroked his fullness first with her hand and then her tongue.

'That's enough,' he muttered then, easily reversing their positions so that now he was straddling her, the offending briefs tossed carelessly aside. 'I'm only human,' he added roughly, abrading her nipples with his palms as he looked possessively down at her. 'And I need you...so much.'

Ally wanted to say she felt the same, but his lips were on hers again, his tongue plunging deeply into her mouth. He was showing her how much he wanted her, she realised, taking her with his tongue as he intended to take her with his body. His hands had freed her hair from its clip and were now sliding into the damp strands, his fingertips hard and demanding against her scalp.

She could feel him against her thigh, hard, too, and

velvety soft against her leg. When he drew back to suckle at her breast, she reached for him, but, with a moan of anguish, he pushed her hand away.

'I want to be inside you when I spill my seed,' he muttered, trailing a finger down her stomach and her abdomen to probe the moist curls between her legs. 'I want you to be ready.' His lips curved. 'Are you?'

Ally gasped as he stroked the sensitive nub that guarded her womanhood. She had thought she was in control, but she had no control whatsoever where he was concerned. Within seconds, she was panting with the onslaught of a totally uncontrolled orgasm, and she pushed weakly at his fingers, wanting him to take their place.

'Dammit, I've left something in my coat,' he groaned, but Ally wouldn't let him move away.

'We don't need it,' she protested, guessing at once that he was talking about protection. 'I want you. I want to feel you inside me, heat to heat, skin to skin.'

Raul stared at her. 'Are you sure?'

Ally looked up at him. 'If it's what you want, too?'

'It's what I want,' he told her unsteadily, and, with an exclamation of satisfaction, he sheathed himself inside her...

It was after ten o'clock before Ally and Raul got to bed.

Making love on the sofa in the living room had just been the start of an evening that had been a dizzying delight from start to finish. Although that first time had been over much too quickly, there had been other times, in other places, that had left Ally sated and satisfied in every tiny pore.

Raul had seemed insatiable, and by the time they'd made it upstairs to empty Ally's bath and fill another that they'd shared, Ally's legs had been weak and trembling.

He'd made love to her again in the bath, a feat Ally would never have believed he could do, but, sitting across Raul's thighs, sharing long enervating kisses, she had discovered that anything was possible.

He had also proposed to her in the bath and Ally had stared at him incredulously, her heart in her eyes.

'You want to marry me?' she breathed, hardly daring to believe she'd heard him correctly, and Raul couldn't keep the smug grin off his face as he assured her that indeed that was what he wanted to do. 'But—what about your mother?' she protested. 'Won't she be disappointed that you're not marrying someone younger?'

Raul dipped his tongue into her ear. 'My mother and father know exactly what I want to do,' he said softly. 'I told them weeks ago. Before you came to Finisterre, to be precise.'

Ally's mouth opened. 'Is that true?'

'I thought you might have guessed,' he agreed. 'Why else do you think my parents were so eager to meet you?'

Ally shook her head dazedly. 'I can hardly believe it.'

'So?' Raul prompted. 'Will you marry me? Or must I do as my ancestors did and kidnap you first?'

Ally's lips twitched. 'I think you kidnapped me that night in London,' she admitted ruefully. 'I haven't been able to think of anyone but you since.'

'I wish you'd told me,' said Raul fervently. 'Instead of letting me think you were going to go back to Jeff.'

Ally draped her arms around his neck. 'That reminds me,' she whispered. 'You never did tell me how you found out that Jeff and I weren't back together.'

'Julia told me,' said Raul surprisingly. 'Apparently you'd written to Suzanne when you got back to thank her for letting you stay, and it was obvious from your letter that you and your ex-husband were not planning a reconciliation.'

'Oh. Oh, yes.' Ally had forgotten writing that letter. Suzanne hadn't bothered to reply, but Ally had felt she owed it to the other woman to do the polite thing. After all, it wasn't Suzanne's fault that things hadn't turned out as she'd planned. She bit her lips. 'So—are you saying that Julia knows about us?'

'I think she has a fairly good idea,' remarked Raul drily. 'Carlos isn't known for his discretion and he's known for some time.'

Ally cupped his face with her hands. 'Then thank heavens for that,' she breathed. 'I do love you, you know.'

'And I love you,' he echoed, enjoying the freedom to touch her whenever, and wherever, he liked. 'Did I tell you how delicious you are? How seductive you look sitting there, with only a few soapsuds for cover?'

Ally's cheeks turned pink. 'Who, me?'

'You,' he conceded huskily. 'I can't wait to take you back to San Cristobál.'

Ally hesitated. 'Suzanne's not going to be very pleased.'

'Hey, who cares what Suzanne thinks? After crying on your shoulder, she didn't even bother to tell you when her financial troubles were over.'

'Well, I think I can understand that,' said Ally generously. 'She was so proud when she thought Julia was going to marry you. She would have hated to tell me it was all off.'

Raul shrugged. 'If you say so.'

'I do say so.' Ally's blush deepened. 'You're a very attractive man.'

'Soon to be a very attractive *married* man?' he asked pointedly, and she dimpled.

'Soon to be a very attractive married man,' she agreed, and Raul covered her smiling lips with his.

Ally rang Sam before going to bed.

Raul proved he wasn't averse to turning his hand to anything if he had to, and, while he was whipping them up a couple of Spanish omelettes, Ally phoned her daughter.

Sam seemed totally unsurprised to hear from her mother. 'Is he there?' she asked eagerly, and Ally agreed that he was. 'Are you going to marry him?' Sam added, as soon as her mother had assured herself that her daughter had indeed rung Raul at the Post House, and she gasped.

'How do you know about that?'

'I asked him what his intentions were, of course,' declared Sam unrepentantly. 'By the way, I phoned Ryan and told him, too. He said you had his blessing, for what it's worth.'

'But how could you—?' Ally forced herself not to go any further. 'Don't you mind?'

'Mind?' Sam snorted. 'Mum, it's the best thing that could have happened to you. What's to mind?'

Ally mentioned her daughter's reaction to Raul as they got into her bed later. Sam had said she was spending the night at Mark's—to 'give them space', as she put it—and Raul was only too happy not to have to go back to the hotel.

'She's a good kid,' he said, settling her spoonwise into the curve of his thighs, her back against his chest. 'I hope she and your son realise that they'll always have a home with us, whatever they choose to do with their lives.'

Ally lifted her hand and drew his head down onto her shoulder. 'I'm never going to sleep,' she said shakily. 'I'm so excited; so elated; so—so afraid this is all a dream.'

'It's no dream,' Raul assured her, nuzzling her neck. 'But, if you're not tired, I think I know of something that might help...'

# EPILOGUE

ALLY stretched luxuriously and got up from the cushioned lounger just as her husband came out of the sliding French doors onto the patio at Finisterre. Raul had accompanied his father to San Cristóbal, to visit the marina, and the older man followed his son onto the terrace.

'Ally, my dear,' he exclaimed, bestowing a warm caress on her cheek before Raul could slip his arm about her waist and pull her close for a lingering kiss. 'I am sorry we have been so long. Has Isabel outstayed her welcome?'

'Isabel couldn't outstay her welcome,' asserted Ally firmly, nodding to where her mother-in-law and their other guests were gathered around the barbecue at the other end of the terrace. 'She's so good with Sam and Ryan. She treats them as if they really are her grandchildren.'

'They are our grandchildren,' retorted Juan fiercely. 'They're your children, aren't they, Ally? And you know how fond we are of you. How could we not love your children, too?'

Ally looked up at Raul with eyes that were suddenly moist. 'You're all so kind,' she whispered. 'You've made me so happy.'

'You've made me happy, *querida*,' responded Raul, using the Spanish endearment as he sometimes did when they were alone together. Then, even though Ally knew he wished they were alone together, he said, 'What are they doing?'

'It looks like your mother is showing the young people how to barbecue the fish Maria bought in San Cristóbal this morning,' remarked Juan, sauntering across the terrace to where Ally's daughter, Sam, and her new husband, Mark, were gathered with Ryan and his girlfriend, Penny, around his wife. '*Hola,*' he cried. 'What's going on?'

Watching him, Raul drew Ally closer. 'Are you really happy?' he asked huskily, and she punched him lightly in the ribs.

'Stop fishing for compliments,' she said, knowing he was teasing her. After a year of marriage, she thought she knew her husband very well, and she still marvelled at how happy they were together. 'Did you see Carlos?'

'Yeah. He and Julia will be along later. It depends how she's feeling. You know how uncomfortable the first three months of a pregnancy can be.'

Ally nodded. 'Mmm,' she conceded reminiscently. 'Don't I just? But it's worth it.'

'Is it?' Raul touched her cheek, and she gave a soft laugh.

'I think so.' Then, because they were becoming too involved with each other, she forced herself to look away, and said, 'How do you think your mother is?'

'Pretty good, I think,' said Raul manfully, accepting that for the present they couldn't abandon their guests. 'Since she and Dad don't have this big place to be responsible for, she's looked less tired. Dad's idea of building a smaller house on the grounds was a good one.'

'You don't think she misses it?'

'Misses this place?' Raul gave her an old-fashioned look. 'What are you saying? She's never away.' He broke off as he heard footsteps behind them. 'And here comes the reason why she can't bear to tear herself away.' His eyes were drawn to his wife's full breasts swelling above the rounded neckline of her cream silk blouse. 'Has he been fed?'

Ally chuckled, knowing how much Raul liked to watch her feeding their three-month-old son, and, turning, she took the baby from the nanny's arms. 'I'm afraid so,' she said, looking down into the child's smiling face. 'Can't you tell?'

'Is that the smile I wear after you've satisfied me?' asked

her husband slyly, and Ally reached up to brush his lips with hers.

'Exactly the same,' she assured him. 'Here: take your son. He's getting too heavy for me to carry around.'

Raul didn't believe her, but he took the baby Manuel obediently enough, cradling him in his arms with an ease born of frequent experience. From the very beginning, when Ally had first discovered she was pregnant, Raul had always been there for her, helping her and supporting her every step of the way. She knew he'd been anxious about her pregnancy, but when he'd realised she was delighted about it, he'd said no more. And there was no doubt that he was extremely proud of them both.

'Hey, look who's here!'

Sam had just seen her baby brother in his father's arms and, leaving the others, she came sauntering across to fuss over him. Although she'd told her mother that she had no intention of having any children for at least five years, there was an obvious look of envy in her eyes as she touched the baby's soft cheek.

'Ah, the *niño*!' Isabel Ramirez wasn't far behind her, and she slipped an arm around Sam's shoulders as they both smiled at the little boy.

'Take him,' said Raul, when it became obvious that Sam was itching to do so, and Ryan, who had come to see what all the fuss was about, pulled a resigned face.

'Women,' he said, giving his mother a teasing smile. 'What is it about women and babies that gets them every time?'

'You'll find out,' remarked Raul drily, drawing Ally away from the group, which had now increased to include Mark and Penny. He bent to murmur in her ear. 'Do you think we'd be missed?'

Ally's laugh was infectious. 'You're incorrigible,' she

said, feeling his thumb brush the underside of her breast, and he gave a rueful sigh.

'Just in love,' he corrected her softly. 'But I suppose I can wait. I've got the rest of my life to show you what you mean to me...'

## HARLEQUIN *Super*ROMANCE®

### The GUARDIANS

**An action-packed new trilogy by**

# Kay David

**This time the good guys wear black. Join this highly skilled SWAT team as they serve and protect Florida's Emerald Coast.**

**#960 THE NEGOTIATOR**
(January 2001)

**#972 THE COMMANDER**
(March 2001)

**#985 THE LISTENER**
(May 2001)

**Look for these
Harlequin Superromance titles
coming soon to your favorite
retail outlet.**

## HARLEQUIN®
*Makes any time special* ™

# LONG, TALL TEXANS

## EMMETT, REGAN & BURKE

*New York Times*
extended list bestselling author

## Diana PALMER

**returns to Jacobsville, Texas, in this special
collection featuring rugged heroes, spirited
heroines and passionate love stories told
in her own inimitable way!**

*Coming in May 2001 only from Silhouette Books!*

## Silhouette®

*Where love comes alive*™

Visit Silhouette at www.eHarlequin.com

PSLLT

**He's** a man of cool sophistication.
**He's** got pride, power and wealth.
He's a ruthless businessman, an expert lover—
and he's one hundred percent committed
to staying single.

Until now. Because suddenly he's responsible
for a BABY!

# HIS BABY

An exciting miniseries from Harlequin Presents®
**He's sexy, he's successful...
and now he's facing up to fatherhood!**

On sale February 2001:
RAFAEL'S LOVE-CHILD
by Kate Walker, Harlequin Presents® #2160

On sale May 2001:
MORGAN'S SECRET SON
by Sara Wood, Harlequin Presents® #2180

And look out for more later in the year!

*Available wherever Harlequin books are sold.*

HARLEQUIN®
*Makes any time special* ™

Visit us at www.eHarlequin.com

HPBABY

# INDULGE IN A QUIET MOMENT
## WITH HARLEQUIN

### Get a FREE

*Quiet Moments Bath Spa*

## with just two proofs of purchase from
## any of our four special collector's editions in May.

---

**Harlequin® is sure to make your time special this Mother's Day
with four special collector's editions featuring a short story
*PLUS* a complete novel packaged together in one volume!**

Collection #1  Intrigue abounds in a collection featuring *New York Times*
bestselling author Barbara Delinsky and Kelsey Roberts.

Collection #2  Relationships? Weddings? Children? = *New York Times*
bestselling author Debbie Macomber and Tara Taylor Quinn
at their best!

Collection #3  Escape to the past with *New York Times* bestselling author
Heather Graham and Gayle Wilson.

Collection #4  Go West! With *New York Times* bestselling author
Joan Johnston and Vicki Lewis Thompson!

## *Plus Special Consumer Campaign!*
Each of these four collector's editions will feature a
"FREE QUIET MOMENTS BATH SPA" offer.
See inside book in May for details.

### Only from

**HARLEQUIN®**
*Makes any time special*®

**Don't miss out! Look for this exciting promotion on sale in May 2001,
at your favorite retail outlet.**

Visit us at www.eHarlequin.com                    PHNCP01

## Getting down to business in the boardroom... and the bedroom!

A secret romance, a forbidden affair, a thrilling attraction...

What happens when two people work together and simply can't help falling in love—no matter how hard they try to resist?

Find out in our new series of stories set against working backgrounds.

### Look out for

### THE MISTRESS CONTRACT
by Helen Brooks, Harlequin Presents® #2153
Available January 2001

### and don't miss

### SEDUCED BY THE BOSS
by Sharon Kendrick, Harlequin Presents® #2173
Available April 2001

*Available wherever Harlequin books are sold.*

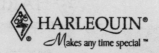

**HARLEQUIN®**
*Makes any time special* ™

Visit us at www.eHarlequin.com

HP925